CW01021174

A Doctor's Tale

by

Stanley Feldman

Grosvenor House
Publishing Limited

About the Author

I gave up working for my biochemistry thesis on the metabolism of the wood louse to study medicine in 1950 as I did not think it was a Nobel Prize winning subject. Qualified (hons) Westminster Medical School 1955. Trained as anaesthetist at Westminster Hosp. Learnt research techniques as a Fulbright Fellow; Univ. Washington USA 1957-58. Snr. Lecturer Postgraduate Med. School, 1962. Advisor in Post Studies Faculty Anaesthetist Royal College Surgeons 1965-1970. Boerhaave adviser University of Leiden1972-1980, Visiting Professor Stanford University USA 1967-1968. Higginbotham Lecturer. Dallas USA, Frederickson Orator. Emory University Atlanta USA.

Member Senate University of London, Chair of Anaesthesia Univ. London at Charing Cross and Westminster Med Schools (later Imperial College School Medicine). Director of Research at the Royal National Orthopaedic Hosp. 1994-97.

Author/Editor; 14 text books in Anaesthesia, including Scientific Foundations of Anaesthesia (4 editions), Mechanism of Action of Drugs; Drugs in Anaesthesia (3 editions); Anatomy for Anaesthetists (10 editions); Muscle Relaxant Drugs (2 editions). etc. Editor Journal, Anaesthetic Pharmacology. Contributor; Encyclopaedia Britannica 1965-6-7.

Published over100 peer reviewed papers on molecular mechanisms of drug action, the evolution of animal life and science education.

Recent publication 'From Poison Arrows to Prozac'.2008 publ. John Blake. Panic Nation (with Vincent Marks) publ. John Blake 2005.2cnd edition 2008. Life Begins. 2007 publ. Metro Books.

Latest book, Global Warming and other Bollocks, with Prof Vincent Marks, published July 2009.

This book is published by
Grosvenor House Publishing Ltd
28-30 High Street, Guildford, Surrey, GU1 3HY.
www.grosvenorhousepublishing.co.uk

A CIP record for this book
is available from the British Library

ISBN 978-1-907211-92-8

Acknowledgements

My tale would not have been written but for the insistence of my colleagues who, like me, have many happy memories of our particular time in medicine and felt that, in the rapidly changing world of 'The Hospital' there should be a record of 'what it used to be like'.

I would like to pay tribute to the doctors and nurses with whom I have had the pleasure to work. Had we not all shared the common goal of seeing that our patients received the best treatment we could offer, no matter what the personal cost, then many of the events chronicled in this book would not have occurred and we would not be able to look back at those times with so much pleasure and satisfaction.

I would like to acknowledge the enormous part played by the theatre staff, who in their report described me as 'quick but messy' and who have tolerated my idiosyncrasies with benign fortitude.

In particular, I would like to pay a special tribute to Carole, my wife, who has inspired me, cajoled me and who has participated in so many of the events described in this book. Without her help this book would probably not have been written.

I was fortunate in being able to bully my good friends, Vivette Dallas and Ahmet Orge, who thought they were going to be on a care free cruise down the Irrawaddy river, to give up some of their sunshine hours to copy edit the manuscript-if it had it not been for their efforts there would have had many more errors in the text!

Stanley Feldman 2010.

Contents

Introduction

I was pronounced dead in 2008.

It was when I met a colleague from down under who stared at me as though he had seen a ghost that I discovered that my obituary had been published in an Australian medical journal in 2008.

It is sobering to have advance warning of one's demise but it prompted me to set about recording some of the many funny tales, (both funny peculiar and funny amusing), of my time in medicine They have formed the basis of this book. Up to that time I had frequently referred to some of the more outrageous events during after dinner talks but in view of the notice of my untimely demise I set about chronicling them with a sense of urgency. The result has been 'A Doctor's Tale'.

I have used a loosely biographical format in order to give some structure to what otherwise would be a series of anecdotes and to give me a chance to give vent to some of my personal, 'grumpy old man', views.

All the stories included in the book are based on fact although some have been dramatised, or the circumstances in which they occurred changed, in order to save the blushes of those involved. If in retelling of these events I have caused offence to any person involved it was unintentional. I regard myself as having been especially fortunate in having colleagues who, as well as being very good doctors, enjoyed a great sense of humour and an ability to laugh at themselves.

It is was not my intention for the title of this book to bring the Canterbury Tales to mind although, as in Chaucer's stories, it is the chronicle of someone with a tale to tell. Like the Canterbury tales it is intended to amuse and entertain and to give the reader a peep into what life was like in bygone days.

Chapter One

In the Beginning

I used to think I was born at the age of nine. I have so few memories of anything that happened before that time that I seemed to have missed out on being a child. As I sit here looking at a photograph of myself as a youngster, in the second row of pupils at the Burdett-Coutts primary school in Westminster, it brings back hazy memories of those school days. I have fleeting recollections of parading around the playground on St George's day, many years ago, to the tune of 'An English Country Garden' played on the old upright school piano. Perhaps the grudging smile on my face in the picture is a premonition of life's paradoxes. There we were, solemnly saluting the Union flag, in that small dark, barren concrete yard, surrounded by high brick walls in the centre of the urban wilderness of Westminster. Although we were singing at the top of our voices about the joys of the flowers in an English country garden most of the children were totally ignorant of these pleasures as they had never ventured far from the local Peabody Estate that was their home.

Now, looking back on those days it is the odd events; the funny things that happened that are most readily recalled. Anxieties, that appeared disastrous at the time, have become unimportant, even amusing when one's life is viewed through the wrong end of the telescope of time.

An Evacuee

I was nine, coming up for ten, when war broke out. It may well have been the psychological trauma and the worry about the inevitability of the impending tragedy that jogged my memory into existence at that time. Even today, I can remember the increasing anxiety and gloom that accompanied the build up to the war in the summer of 1939. The men filling sandbags, the family gathering around the wireless, anxious to hear every news broadcast, the preparation for mobilisation, the ARP (air raid protection) posters, the issuing of gas masks and the gas drills; all culminating in that broadcast on Sept 3rd 1939 announcing that- 'today we are at war'. There were the whispered conversations about 'evacuation'. With them came the realisation that our lives were about to be abruptly changed, our family was to be split up and my sister and I were to be separated from our Mum and Dad. We were entering a new era, one of uncertainty and loss.

After many anguished discussion my parents decided that it would be better if both of their children were evacuated together. Most schools at that time were single sex institutions. As a result my sister and I attended different neighbourhood schools which meant that we were quite likely to be evacuated to different parts of the country. This would have caused an enormous logistic problem for my parents making it difficult for them to make regular visits to both of us. It was decided that the solution was for us both to be registered at the same school. So it was that I became a temporary girl, a member of the rather snooty Grey Coat Hospital School for Girls. I was not the only male in the school, there were two other boys who, as I now recall, were much older than me; possibly even 12 or 13 years old.

It was on a sad September day that we set out on a journey into the unknown of 'evacuation'. Clutching our one bag per child and our cardboard box containing our gas mask, we set off from Victoria Station. No one knew our destination or those that did weren't telling. I remember arriving at our new school towards evening that day and seeing it standing all by itself, surrounded by rolling green lawns and trees. We had arrived at our safe haven, at a famous girl's public School, in Brighton.

It was obviously a shock to our hosts to find that, in addition to the large influx of girls, there were three young persons, who were wearing trousers. It fell to them to look after us until homes could be found for us in the neighbouring communities. It was not an easy job to persuade the suspicious local families to take in unknown children from London as by and large London children had an undeserved reputation for being difficult, dirty urchins. However, with the promise of extra ration books, volunteers were slowly coming forward to meet the challenge. This did not solve the school's present problem, how to accommodate the three ugly ducklings, the three boys, in a girls' school. I can remember the confusion as the three of us were segregated, given supper and put to bed in a small room off the main hall; I think it was probably the sanatorium. It was one of the older boys who found the notice over our beds; the cause of our fall from grace, it read 'If in the night you need a mistress press this bell'. As very much the youngest of the trio it was only many years later that I came to understand why the other boys found ringing the bell to be so funny.

The very next day we were moved out of Rodean. It was to be the start of my peripatetic school career. It was not long before the German bombers found the English coast and the sound of anti-aircraft guns kept us awake at nights. At first I was sent to a council school but when that was considered to be too far away from our temporary accommodation, another rather posh school, where Latin was de rigueur, was found for me. Unfortunately I did not stay long enough to master the elements of this subject, a lapse I was to come to regret in later life. From Brighton to Dunstable; from Dunstable back to London, from London to South Wales and then to Luton. It seemed that whenever I settled down in a new school someone in Hitler's high command would know. Off would go the bombers with the result there would be another move, yet one more new school.

Eventually, completely fed up with the disruption to my schooling, my parents decided that it was time to return to London. It was time for the chaps in the German high command to get busy once again; it was the time of the buzz bombs and V2 rockets. It was 1944-45.

Schools at War

Towards the end of the war those schools that remained operational in London were kept open by a makeshift staff of retired teachers and part time volunteers. My school in London was the Sloane School in Chelsea.

It had a very restricted range of teachers none of whom taught mathematics or science. As my interest lay in science I found it necessary to pursue the greater part of my studies at Chelsea Polytechnic evening classes. At the age of sixteen I found myself spending four nights every week, from 6.0pm until 9.0 pm, at the polytechnic, in addition to attending regular day school. Whilst far from ideal, Chelsea Polytechnic introduced me to an academic environment and to true scholarship. Many of the teachers were recruited from the University of London colleges that had been bombed and were no longer operational. Most of the students were mature and many held down working jobs during the day. At that time Chelsea was very much an art college with its famous Chelsea Arts Club and its New Year Eve Art's Club Ball but it had good departments in biological sciences and physics. It was to be my initiation into a grown up world.

It was whilst I was at the Chelsea Polytechnic that I became interested in research, in knowing why and how the systems that keep living things alive worked. I set about solving the puzzle of how bivalves, two shell molluscs, like the oyster and mussel, keep the two parts of their shell closed, defying brute force and the advantage of leverage and of how fish managed to obtain sufficient oxygen to meet their needs from the little that is dissolved in water. As a result of the enthusiasm I had displayed in these studies I was co-opted as the note taker onto a small committee that was formed towards the end of the war to investigate the weevil infestation of flour. I remember that the committee came to the considered view that to remove the weevil contamination would be inadvisable as, at that time, it constituted a significant contribution to the protein intake in the diet of the population. Although the protein ration per person had been carefully calculated no allowance had been made for the army of pets kept by the British who sacrificed their precious rations to keep their pets well nourished. The decision of the committee was kept a secret from the public lest they stopped eating bread!

Once I obtained my degree it was suggested that I carried on in research for a PhD degree. I was flattered and eager to start on my thesis but my enthusiasm was deflated by the subject that was chosen; it was to be on the nitrogen metabolism of the wood louse! How did the animal build up its bodily protein if it lived in an environment devoid of nitrogen and composed entirely of cellulose?

My adolescent visions of Nobel Prize ceremonies, of saving lives, of public lectures and honours; all seemed a long way off from the protein metabolism of the wood louse. If I was to win fame and fortune, if I was to become a new Pasteur or Currie, I had to try a different tack. I decided I would become a doctor.

The Doctor's Tale

It was not easy to get into Medical School at the end of the war as a minimum of seventy percent of student places were reserved for those returning from the armed forces. Fortunately, there were no qualms about giving the majority of the remaining places to men rather than to women. The Women's Liberation Movement and the Equal Rights laws had yet to make any impact on those selecting the future doctors and dentists for the country. Indeed many Deans were unabashed misogynists. One

Dean explained that he believed that if a girl was good looking she did not need a career in medicine if not, then medicine wasn't enough! Their prejudice gave me a chance of a place in this highly competitive system. I was fortunate to win a scholarship to Westminster Medical School to start training to be a doctor in 1951. I was twenty one years old.

Like several other ancient medical establishments, Westminster Medical School had no pre-clinical teaching facilities. This meant studying anatomy, physiology and biochemistry at the nearby Kings College in the Strand.

King's College London

In the post war era most Medical Schools were a mix of MASH and Doctor in the House. The large numbers of ex-service students created a racy environment of mature men who had many years experience of army life. Many were heavy drinkers who were always ready to 'have a go'. They were bloody minded and not easily brow beaten by the urbane superiority of eminent, successful consultants, who, with their large Harley Street practices and equally large incomes, were more used to dealing with errant servants than ex-soldiers. But, before one qualified to walk the wards with the 'Sir Lancelot Spraggs' of the medical establishment, there was anatomy, physiology and biochemistry to master.

We were divided up into groups of three in the anatomy department at Kings College. Each group was designated to work on a particular part of a formalin smelling, leathery coated shrunken corpse. Contrary to popular belief the bodies appeared totally inanimate and were treated as such. There were few ribald jokes and little if any inappropriate treatment of the bodies; they could just as well been made of wax. Each group of three students set about dissecting a limb or the abdomen, the thorax or the head and neck. One of the group would hold the dissection manual and read out the instructions, whilst the other two would take turns with the scalpel and forceps. Every nerve, fibre, muscle and tendon were carefully separated and displayed so that a mental note of its origins, destination and position, relative to other structures, were noted. Each week a demonstrator, usually a surgeon in training, would test us on what we had learnt.

After the bodies were dissected and reduced to their basic bits and pieces, each carcass was returned to its particular wooden box but as it had to weigh the same as it did when it was delivered, there was invariably a hunt around for 'make weight' pieces of wood and bone before the box lid was finally sealed down.

Today, human body dissection is no longer part of the anatomy class syllabus in most medical schools. It is a pity for there is no doubt that the appreciation of the relationships of the various structures of which the body is made up has been knowledge that has been invaluable to me, and to many of my colleagues, in our different careers. The idea that only surgeons need to know anatomy denies present day doctors an essential insight into the way our bodies are put together.

Our anatomy group consisted of an ex-service, tank commander with a gammy leg, Brian, a super fit athletic product of a Grammar School and me. Amongst the other teams working on our body I remember Roy best. He was an ex-army captain whose father was a doctor. In June that year Roy had been accepted for Medical School to start in September but he had found the commanding officer of his army unit, stationed in the Far East, unsympathetic to his pleas for an early release from the service. Frustrated and cross he had spent a weekend leave with two friends in neighbouring Hong Kong. They had all got terribly drunk and on his way back to their base on the Star Ferry he had thrown most of the life belts overboard. At the subsequent court of inquiry he was asked the rather silly question, 'what made you do it', to which he replied, that he 'could not bear to see all the little fish drowning'. To his delight he was punished by being dishonourably discharged from the army- in time for him to start his medical career.

Another ex- army student was the little Welshman, Garry. Like many of the students Garry's life revolved around rugby. Although he pursued his studies enthusiastically from Monday to Friday, his life really centred around rugby. On Saturday he was to be found on the sports ground, as scrum half for one or other Welsh rugby team. This was invariably followed by a night of heavy drinking. His Sunday's were devoted to God, nursing his hangover in a local Chapel, so that he would be fit for his studies on Monday.

Brian, the star athlete of our group, was soon part of the College cricket and rugby teams. He spent every Wednesday afternoon training at the College grounds at Cobham. It so happened that Wednesday was also a time set aside for dissection. In his absence, we set about dissecting the body with gusto. Unfortunately, too often this left Brian with little more than gristle and bone to examine when he returned to the college on the following day. To this day he attributes his decision to take up orthopaedic surgery and his success, as one of the leading lights of the speciality, to having missed out as a medical student on the anatomy of almost everything, except bones, joints and gristle.

I remember our physiology professor. He was a stocky, bad tempered man. Perhaps his unsympathetic persona owed something to the uncompromising put down he received when he published his life's work, a book titled 'Sane Psychiatry'. The review was short and to the point 'this is neither sane nor psychiatry'. The ex-servicemen in our group lost no time in displaying enlarged copies of the review around the College.

Although my time at King's was academically uninspiring as it involved a lot of 'learning by rote' rather than by enquiry and investigation, it did lead to friendships that have persisted to this day.

Somehow, all but a handful of the students managed to scrape through the 2cnd MB examination. With this hurdle behind us we had our pass to the world of the hospital ward and real patients.

Chapter Two

Hospital Life

The Teaching Hospital of the 1950s was a very different place from any hospital today. It was a place run by the doctors for the benefit of their patients. There was a pervasive atmosphere of learning and self importance. Whether a patient, a doctor, a medical student or a nurse, you were made to feel privileged to have been granted entry to the portals of such an august academy of learning. The Teaching Hospitals were distinctly superior to the ordinary hospitals with their institutional, civic atmosphere. Unlike today's hospitals, with their large administrative machinery and their attendant army of clip board personnel, checking on targets and auditing performance, they were administered by a small staff all of whom were proud to be part of the Institution and its history. The administration consisted of the Hospital Secretary and his Assistant, a Bursar, a Financial director and a Supervisor of Works, together with their secretaries. All the members of the administration demonstrated an unswerving allegiance to the Hospital, its reputation and to its doctors and nurses. This made them as faithful and reliable as any family retainer on a nobleman's estate. All the members of the hospital staff, whether they were medical or administrative, were indulgent to the medical students; their 'young gentlemen', turning out to support them in inter- hospital rugby matches and willing co-conspirators in any student rag. There was a Board of Governors made up of distinguished, usually wealthy, personalities, who served in a voluntary capacity. Together with the hospital secretary they oversaw the general finances of the hospital and helped in the frequent fund raising events. The day to day administration of the hospital was in the hands of a committee of senior consultants. The consultants were important men. They were at the very pinnacle of their careers. As they could advance no further in medicine they often devoted much of their time to promoting their hospital and its students. They would arrive from Harley Street in their chauffeur driven limousines to be met at the portal of the hospital by their houseman, the most junior doctor in their team. He would help the great man, (never a women) off with his overcoat, take his hat and case in his arms and convey this 'lord of medicine', accompanied by his retinue of ward sister, registrars, housemen and students, to the outpatient department, ward or operating theatre.

One famous senior surgeon from a neighbouring medical school who was attending a meeting at the Royal College of Surgeons towards the end of the war caused a stir when, at the end of the talk, observations from the audience were invited. At this point he rose to his feet and embarked upon a lengthy recital of his army rank and his numerous hospital appointments followed by a list of the important committees on which he served. At this point the audience, embarrassed by his blatant self-promotion, started to become restless. He continued by giving the following explanation for his intervention.

He said that when he had arrived, someone in front of him had turned to his neighbour and said quite loudly 'who is that funny looking bugger who's just come in'! Senior surgeons in those days were important people and expected to be instantly recognisable and their importance universally appreciated.

In the hierarchy of consultants, the surgeon was king. He wielded the right of life or death for his patients by virtue of the scalpel that he held in his hand. Next came the physician, usually in order of seniority, unless one of their number had treated royalty or had been knighted, in which case his position in the pecking order of importance was enhanced. Obstetricians, anaesthetist and those serving less dramatic specialities, such as skins or eyes were usually accorded a less formal greeting.

It was unusual for there to be less than two or three knights of the realm amongst the staff, a status more often accorded to them as a result of whom they had treated, or for a post they had held in a Learned College, than for any major contribution to the advancement of medicine. This was not to say they did not contribute to the research or new ideas. To the contrary, it was because of their dominance in their particular field of medicine it often fell to them to introduce a new treatment or a radical idea. In my time at Westminster Medical School it's doctors introduced one of the earliest successful techniques of open heart surgery for babies and children, new methods of anaesthesia that made surgery possible without undue blood loss, the first donor kidney transplant, the first bone marrow transplant, new techniques of radio-therapy, the vascular pedicle technique for facial reconstruction after cancer surgery and many less dramatic contributions that had doctors from all over the world coming to learn how to perform these medical innovations. They were exciting times. Inevitably there was huge competition to join the junior staff and to learn the craft at the feet of the masters. Not only had the aspiring doctor to demonstrate his medical prowess, he also had to 'fit in'. They were the power houses of new ideas in medicine. As such, it was only to be expected that they included in their numbers more than their share of eccentrics and prima donnas.

By the 1950s, the medical hierarchy was under strain as newly appointed consultants, returning from years spent in the services, who were less affluent and as a result more amenable to the erosion of their status by the seeds of egalitarianism that crept in with the advent of the National Health Service.

This effect also involved the nursing staff. After all, only 40 years earlier, before the first World War, a girl (almost invariably from a middle class home) who chose to become a trainee nurse at one of the great London teaching hospitals, would either have paid for her board and keep or, as was the case at St Thomas' Hospital and Westminster Hospital, charged for their training. In those days nurses worked six days a week. They were encouraged to use their day off, either to make their own uniform (material usually provided by the hospital) or for religious devotions. Even as late as 1955, Nightingale nurses at the nearby St Thomas' Hospital were not permitted to speak to a doctor until he had first addressed them. They were obliged always to address him as 'doctor'. By the late

1950s nursing had become a more open profession, even in the teaching hospitals. It was available to any who were suitably able and was no longer restricted to middle class 'gals'. As it provided a way in which 'the right sort of gal' could meet up with an aspiring doctor there was considerable competition for nursing posts in the teaching hospitals of the day.

The Matron's primary duty was the protection of her nurses and making sure that the patients did what they were told. She wielded great power and even the senior surgeons walked in fear of her. She ruled the wards through her acolytes, the ward sisters. Woe betide any student who crossed the ward sister, he became a pariah and his life was made miserable. Even the consultant could not intercede to save him from sister's wrath. They controlled the day to day running of the ward. They made sure the patients received the best treatment possible, even if this occasioned them to intercede on the behalf of a patient with the consultant in charge if they felt the treatment was inappropriate. It was they who made sure the ward was properly cleaned and the food was up to standard. They had the power to hire or fire any recalcitrant nurse, maid or orderly. Today they have lost that power because they work in shifts.

When I first arrived at the medical school the Dean was a distinguished physician of the old school, Sir Adolph Abrahams. His brother was Harold Abrahams the 1938 Olympic medallist of Chariots of Fire fame. The only times I saw him were in the library where Adolph, always attired in his pin striped trousers and the black jacket that were de rigueur for a gentleman of his distinction, would invariably be reading the morning papers-even at 3.0 pm in the afternoon. When his brother joined him there he would hold forth, like any grumpy old man, on any topical inequity or on how far the personal habits, or the dress, of the students had degenerated since his times. Unfortunately they were both pretty deaf so that their quiet, private conversations would echo, at high decibel level, around the hallowed quiet of the library, much to the amusement of the students

Sir Adolph was followed by Dean Harding, a handsome, approachable orthopaedic surgeon who was a bachelor and a misogynist. I never came to know his first name as he was always fondly known as 'Dean'. He was totally different from his predecessor. Whereas Sir Adolph was aloof, Dean Harding was one of the boys. He enjoyed their jokes and the sense of fun and high spirits. On one occasion, when he was attending a rather drunken party, at a flat occupied by a group of senior students, there was a police raid. A neighbour had complained about the noise and suggested the house was being used as a brothel. The Dean was smuggled down the back stairs as the police came in. The next day he was in office to receive an official complaint from the local constabulary. He assured them, with due solemnity, that appropriate steps would be taken to punish the offenders.

The Deans of the Medical Schools were always on the look out for potential donors who would endow a new facility for the school. So it was that the Dean of a near by medical school readily agreed to host a visiting Arab potentate and his retinue to lunch before accompanying them, in their limousine, to the Inter-hospital rugby match. Amidst champagne and savouries, promises of life long friendship and support were exchanged. It was only when the 'before and after' pictures were printed in the College magazine that the Dean recognised the Sultan as one of his own students and the retinue as students from other medical schools, all in flowing hired fancy dress.

The Surgeons

The senior surgeon at Westminster Hospital was Sir Stanford Cade. If the surgeons were the kings of the medical fraternity, Sir Stanford was their Emperor. He had been born in Russia and educated in Belgium. He never lost his guttural foreign accent or his old world charm. He was a famous cancer surgeon with a prodigious memory and a terrifying bedside manner. He was a pioneer of radium treatment for cancer and he carried a tin tobacco box, full of radium needles, in the back pocket of his trousers. When the occasion arose he would select some of them for insertion into a patient's inoperable tumour. From time to time one of the radio-active needles would fall on the theatre floor necessitating the theatre staff scrabbling around on their hands and knees to find them. They would be retrieved and picked up with unprotected hands, washed under running water from a tap and replace in his tin box. Neither Sir Stanford, nor any of the staff ever suffered from any ill effects of exposure to the radio-activity. Today such an event would set off a full scale radiation alert and would result in the immediate evacuation of the operating theatre.

Sir Stanford was a legend in himself. Once he embarked on something he would not rest content until he was the acknowledge master of the subject. It is told that within a year of taking up stamp collecting he pointed out a forgery on sale at a stamp auction. Within two days of seeing his first case of the rare skin disease, Kaposi sarcoma (now seen quite commonly in patients with HIV) he had read every paper published on it, irrespective of the original language. He was said to obtain the figures for the outcome of his surgery from the obituary columns of the Times newspaper which he read avidly, every day from cover to cover. If Lady X's obituary was not there she was noted down as having survived his surgery and presumed to be still be alive.

He was a tireless, terrier like, surgeon. He knew no bounds when there was a cancer to be excised. He would go on cutting out bits of the patient's anatomy until all signs of tumour were extirpated. He was said to have once remarked that 'there is no tumour too big that if you pull hard enough it won't came away'. He was a pioneer of pelvic evisceration, colloquially known as the hemi-humanectomy for extensive cancer involving pelvic structures. It involved removing the bladder, rectum, the uterus and vagina and any part of the pelvic skeleton that the cancer had invaded.

He expected total commitment and enthusiasm from his staff. Once you became Sir Stanford's houseman you signed on for six months of indented labour. There were no weekends off, no half days and no holidays. Often his operating sessions would not end before midnight. On one occasion a houseman complained to Sir Stanford that he felt unwell and asked if he could have a weekend off. Sir Stanford replied 'by all means, but if you go don't bother to come back'. That weekend the unfortunate houseman perforated his gastric ulcer and found himself undergoing surgery. Sir Stanford remained convinced that he did it deliberately to undermine his authority. That particular houseman was persuaded to give up his ambition for a career in surgery.

As a reward for this dedication his staff found Sir Stanford to be a loyal chief who went out of his way to help establish the careers of those who had worked for him and had shown promise.

Following the death of his wife from cerebral malaria, whilst they were on a trip to South Africa, Sir Stanford became a lonely figure, totally absorbed in medicine. He would often invite his junior staff to his home in Harley Street after a long operating session and feed them on caviar and champagne. He would enquire about their families and their medical aspirations and ambitions. He would keep them talking until the early hours of the morning. He seemed to need no sleep. Indeed, on one occasion, long after he had retired, I met him during a consultation over a private patient when he admitted that he was beginning to feel old as he now needed four hours sleep a night.

Westminster Hospital had a strong team of chest surgeons. When the late King, George sixth had cancer of the lung it was the team from Westminster Hospital that was invited to Buckingham Palace to perform the operation to remove the tumour. The operation was a great success. The surgeon, Clement Price Thomas was knighted for his services. Sir Clement was a fiery Welshman who operated wearing wooden Welsh clogs; woe betide any registrar who got in his way. Sir Clement's heavy clog would deliver a blow to his shins that would

soon cause him to mend his ways. More experienced
registrars soon learned to wear football shin pads under
their socks as a badge of honour. The late King expressed
a wish to be nursed by men as he was rather shy and was
embarrassed by the attention of female nurses. As a
result Sir Clement's registrar was deputed to look after
him. When the young surgical registrar arrived at the
Palace carrying a paper bag that contained his personal
luggage, he announced his presence with the immortal
words 'where are the ladies in waiting I am the man they
have been waiting for'. He was the only member of the
surgical team not to receive an honour or a gift from the
royal establishment.

In later years that particular registrar became a
consultant chest surgeon at Westminster Hospital. He
soon developed a private practice composed largely of
Greek patients with impossible names. He took to calling
them all Mr Onassis as that was a name he could remember and spell. So it was that on one occasion the operating list which was published the evening before the
following day's surgery contained the information that a
Mr Onassis was to have his lung removed for cancer.
Unbeknown to the staff, one of the hospital porters had
established a profitable side line by informing the press
of important people who were having operations at
Westminster Hospital. The news that Mr Onassis was
to undergo surgery for cancer soon hit the headlines-
followed by a rapid denial from the office of the Greek
shipping magnate, who at that time, was married to
Jacqueline Kennedy.

Miles Foxen was a distinguished ear nose and throat
surgeon. He was a good, thoughtful doctor who had

acquired the epithet of 'gloomy'. His analysis of life was that things are never so bad they can't get worse. I can remember him remarking, after a temporary setback, how it was that every silver lining had a cloud. There was one occasion when he and Sir Stanford Cade had been operating together on a patient with an advanced cancer of the throat. After some hours Sir Stanford announced he had to leave to catch a train to Paris where he was to give a lecture the next day. We eventually finished the operation and retired to the changing room where, to his dismay, Miles found that Sir Stanford had gone off wearing his shoes. He had left his own, rather down at the heel, pair in their place. Miles looked at these poor worn shoes and turned to me with a pitiful look and remarked 'it is not that I particularly mind him going off in my shoes, what really upsets me is that my shoes will be going round Paris without me in them'. Sir Stanford never noticed he was wearing the wrong shoes.

Our cardiac surgeon was Charles Drew. Charles was in the vanguard of open heart surgery. He pioneered the use of a technique to lower body temperature to levels that reduced the oxygen requirements of the various organs to a point were it was safe to stop the heart for a short period. This made it possible to operate upon a non-beating heart rather than one that was actively contracting about 100 times every minute. It was a technique that was particularly valuable in babies and children. In small babies it is very difficult to place stitches, with any degree of accuracy, in a tiny, rapidly beating structure about the size of a small orange. He was a very inventive and caring doctor but when under stress he could be irascible and difficult. In the early days of cardiac surgery every operation was an experiment which carried a failure rate, especially in babies with congenital heart disease. Operations were only carried out on the very sick children for whom not to operate would have meant imminent death. As a result the mortality was inevitably high. It was when one stayed up all night nursing a child after one of these high risk operations, helping its breathing and carefully judging every dose of drug that was administered, that one came to understand the strain that this sort of surgery put upon the surgeon. It was at these moments one understood the tensions that led to the outbursts of emotion in the operating theatre.

The success or failure of early paediatric cardiac surgery often depended on obtaining an accurate diagnosis of the particular defect and how it was affecting the function of the heart. These were pioneering days for paediatric heart surgery and knowledge about the complexities and the variety of the various congenital defects were only slowly being appreciated. Largely as a result of studies that were made on post mortem specimens. To find out the mechanical effect of a particular defect necessitated catheterising the heart and making pressure and flow measurements in its various chambers. This involved inserting a tiny tube through a vein in the thigh and advancing it under x- ray control until it was encouraged to enter the heart. It was a difficult procedure on a tiny baby. It was made even more difficult as initially the procedure had to be carried out in the darkened department. It fell to the anaesthetist to work out some suitable method of putting these desperately ill babies to sleep, in the dark, using a technique that did not change the dynamics of cardio-vascular system. It was as a result of these investigations that the functional disability of babies with unusual heart defects came to be appreciated and a scheme of surgical correction devised. Occasionally emergencies occurred as when the catheter became knotted in one of the chambers of the heart and could not be withdrawn or when it perforated the tiny thin walled appendage of the heart, the auricle of the atria. In spite of these risks no baby died during these extensive investigations in the three years in which I was involved in these studies. This was largely due to the unflappability of the consultant paediatrician who invariably continued to chain smoke cigarettes during the whole of the procedure.

Looking back at those days in the Chest Unit one is struck by the change in the pattern of disease treated in these units over the past 40-50 years. In the 1950s and 1960s, the chest unit at the hospital was one of the largest and busiest departments. Cancer of the lung was so common that we would see about 10 new cases every week. A large proportion of these patients had such bad bronchitis and emphysema, as a result of their smoking, that surgery to remove a lung, or part of it, would have incapacitated them. Instead of surgery, these patients received radiotherapy. The rest were operated upon. We would operate on about 6-7 new patients every week. Although the five year survival of these patients was not very good it was all we had to offer to prolong their lives. The reduction in cigarette smoking and the clean air acts of the 1950s has had a dramatic success in turning this once common lethal diseases into a clinical rarity. As the number of thoracic cases declined so it was replaced by open heart surgery. Until 1958 heart operations were more or less restricted to the surgeon inserting a finger, capped by a small blade, into a beating heart in order to split open a tightly closed, sclerotic valve. The operation of mitral valvotomy. It was in the early 1960s that open heart surgery really took off. In those days it was largely restricted to correcting congenital heart defects and simple valve lesions but as it became more and more successful operations for coronary artery disease became increasingly common. Today many of these procedures have been replaced by non-invasive techniques such as angioplasty and the insertion of stents, although coronary artery bypass surgery still has a part to play.

The Children's Hospital

David Levi was a senior surgeon at the Westminster Children's Hospital. He lived for surgery. He taught anatomy at St Mary's Medical School where his Saturday morning anatomy demonstrations were a 'tour de force' which attracted a large audience. He was ambidextrous. His particular trick was to use both his hands, each holding a piece of chalk, to draw the two sides of the vertebral column at the same time. This feat was always rewarded with a round of applause. He was an old fashioned general surgeon. He would follow an operation to remove a child's tonsils with a prostatectomy on a octogenarian and then with an operation on a baby with pyloric stenosis. He claimed he was a lucky surgeon, as he said of himself 'I am too busy to have complications'. Indeed his complications were very few and far between. He would arrive in the changing room, for a list of several operations, with the command to the nursing staff to 'send for the first two patients'. He would then proceed to remove his suit jacket which had the shirt cuffs attached to the inside of the jacket sleeves. Once down to his trousers and short sleeved shirt (he never removed his collar and tie), he would don a plastic apron and he was ready to operate. In his private practice he was often assisted by the patient's general practitioner as this allowed the GP to charge the patient an 'attendance fee'. These doctors were mostly unused to surgical procedures and the principals of sterility. As a result he would keep them as far from the field of surgery as possible, constantly muttering to himself, 'this is difficult, very difficult' before producing the offending appendix or bowel from the impossibly small wound.

He worked at all hours and on all occassions. Many years after I became a consultant, I used to work with him from time to time. When I congratulated him at his son's wedding reception he whispered to me; 'appendix; John and Liz's Hospital; 6.30'. He seemed to have a special sense that allowed him to know the moment I took off my trousers to get into bed at night for it was then that telephone would ring with a call from him to help at an operation. On one such occasion I found myself confronted with a reluctant, elderly French patient who was unable to pass urine. Unfortunately he spoke no English and my French was very basic. As I approached him with a syringe full of intravenous anaesthetic, miming my intention to inject its content so as to put him to sleep, he leapt out of bed shouting 'no pi pi'. After a short, breathless chase around his bed he was cornered and subdued. It was only after the intervention of an interpreter that we were able to proceed with the operation. There was no question of informed consent!

I have often had cause to regret my inability to communicate freely with foreign patients. There was one occasion when, having anaesthetised a French patient, I went to visit her in the recovery room. She appeared to be in some discomfort and I enquired in my best French, 'Madame, avez vous le douleur'. My accent obviously confounded her for a puzzled expression appeared on her face slowly to be replaced by a look of recognition and she replied 'non monsieur, pas des dollars, seulement sterling'.

The Gordon Hospital

Eric Crook operated at the Westminster Hospital annexe at the Gordon Hospital in the Vauxhall Bridge Road. He was a typical old school, 'gentleman surgeon'. He was the most polite surgeon I ever met. If one arrived late he would waive aside one's apology and instead insist he was at fault for being early. His anaesthetist was of a different type and he had the habit of starting the day by telling a risky joke which Eric would appear to find funny but which one could see actually caused him a great deal of embarrassment. I remember one occasion when Eric was performing an operation whilst teaching the assembled medical students. He pointed out that the blueish colour of the tissue in the wound around an anal fistula was typical of tuberculous inflammation. A few minutes later, when the anaesthetist replaced the oxygen cylinder which had run out with a full one, the patient's tuberculous inflammation miraculously disappeared. Eric was totally non-plussed by the suddenness of the cure.

Perhaps the best known surgeon who operated at the Gordon Hospital was Lawrence Abel. He was a great friend of Dixon Wright, both were superb technical surgeons but both were surgically arrogant and lacking in any bedside manner. Their treatment of patients would not be acceptable today although there are few surgeons who can match their dexterity. They were good surgeons but indifferent doctors. Lawrence Abel would often see his patients for the first time in the anaesthetic room. There the patient, a little groggy from the effect of the premedication, would see the famous surgeon who would be holding his life in his hands. Unfortunately, more often than not, his surgeon would be wearing a white operating shirt top but no trousers; instead he usually had on boxer shorts covered with pictures of bees bearing the words 'I am a busy bee'. Once the patient was on the operating table Lawrence Abel displayed a masterly surgical ability. I never heard a patient complain about his somewhat unusual attire in the operating theatre and his bizarre manner but in those days it was very rare for any patient ever to complain about his surgeon who was generally regarded as a 'God'.

On one occasion, when he was operating upon a private patient who had cancer of the colon, the patient's private GP, who had come to observe the procedure(and collect an assistants fee), remarked casually that he had suspected the patient also had gall stones. Lawrence Abel put his hand up under the patient's rib cage and after a couple of deft snips with the scissors produced the gall bladder which he threw to the GP with the remark 'you can see for yourself if you were right'.

As an anaesthetist he was a difficult surgeon to work.with. He insisted that such was his skills that his patients did not need any intravenous infusions or blood during the operation and, being a god like creature, he usually had his way. This often led to the anaesthetist having to resuscitate a dehydrated, shocked victim, by starting a blood transfusion the moment he left the operating theatre-not always an easy thing to do.

Obstetrics

Our obstetric department was one of the best in London and the private wing was popular and fashionable. There were three excellent consultant obstetricians including Sir Arthur Bell, past President of the College of Gynaecologists and Obstetricians. Sir Arthur was a canny and enthusiastic accoucheur. When encouraging a mother 'to push' he would became totally involved in the birthing process. His face would go scarlet and the veins on his neck and face would bulge out. It was touch and go as to who would give birth first. He was great horse racing man but his staff soon learned not to rely on his 'tips from the horse's mouth'.

The idol of the 'smart set' was Roger de Vere, labelled 'divine de Vere' by a Sunday Newspaper. Always suave and smiling he was an amusing colleague, never lost for a witty riposte. He encouraged his anaesthetist JB. Wyman to introduce the then new technique of epidural anaesthesia, to alleviate the pain of labour, into common UK practice. For many years epidural labours were limited to about two or three practices in London. The other obstetrician who encouraged the use of epidural anaesthesia was Mr. J B. O'Sullivan. His anaesthetist was the very able, Andrew Doughty. When they successfully delivered a male heir to a Middle Eastern potentate, he gave his almost new Rolls Royce to the obstetrician as a token of his gratitude. The anaesthetist, who had administered the epidural and attended the patient assiduously received a cheque for £20.

De Vere was not a great enthusiast for the various new fashions in maternity practice, he had lived through the Grantley Dick Reed era of 'natural childbirth' and saw little merit in birthing pools. On one occasion when a mother- to-be expressed an interest in the le Vosier method of birthing he pointed out that it meant the patient lying in a bath of water in a darkened room listening to music;-yes, she said, she quite liked that idea; he told her it then meant putting the new born baby, covered in the waxy meconium and any bloody or faecal exudates, to her breast immediately so that they could bond; - now she was becoming less enthusiastic and finally he explained that the full process involved eating some of the placenta; to celebrate the event-that settled it, she decided she would be happy with a conventional delivery.

Chapter Three

Medical School

When we arrived at Westminster Hospital we found that the size of our group of students had been increased by the addition of six students who had completed their preclinical studies at Oxford or Cambridge. Of the forty or so students who now made up our intake, about twenty five were ex-service men, the rest were from families in all walks of life. The majority were from Grammar schools or, like me had experienced a vicarious education. I can only recall two students from public schools. Because of the intense competition to gain entry to medical school we represented the top quintile of academic achievement irrespective of the school system in which we had been educated. Medical students were selected from the academic elite of their schools.

There was never any question as to our commitment. We were all devoted to the new social experiment, the NHS. We were determined to devote our life to treating the sick and relieving suffering. It was the NHS that was going to allow us to do so, irrespective of the patient's ability to pay. It was the stuff of an A.J. Cronin novel. We were like priests entering a seminary, we were dedicating our lives to the cause of medicine. We worked hard, we never questioned the hours needed to master the subject. Holidays and weekends were readily sacrificed. Society was giving us the opportunity to do good, to develop the knowledge that would allow us to serve our patients and save then from pain and disease no matter what the cost in terms of time or money. Out of the students who entered medical school with me, not one failed to complete the course, although several took two or three attempts to pass the final examinations, before they qualified. We were the evangelists of the new age of the NHS

It would be misleading to suggest that, as students, we did not let our hair down and have fun but our off duty activities were always subservient to the needs of our studies. We had little money; only a few of us had an allowance from our parents or from a bursary, the majority lived in sordid digs on student grants. One of these digs had become available through the local council at a bargain rental. Two of my colleagues snapped it up only to discover the reason it was so cheap was the smell. A rotting corpse had been found in the loft when the council took it over. The smell persisted long after the body was removed, in spite of buckets of detol and air wick. Many of the local 'digs' were lacking in basic facilities and some shared a single outside loo with other tenants. Not infrequently, after a large evening fluid intake at the local pub, the student would find his nightly perambulation to the outside loo to relieve himself frustrated by the presence of a tramp who had settled there for the night. There were a few occasions to earn a little extra money to supplement one's grant. A popular student job was that of being an 'extra' at the Sadlers Wells opera. It had the additional attraction of providing an opportunity to meet some of the very attractive young ladies in the chorus. After several months of providing groups of students to enjoy this extra curricular activity, it came to an abrupt end one evening after an exceptionally tall student managed to catch the spear he was carrying in the overhead scenery bringing it crashing down on the singers. It brought the show to an premature close. The management decided that in future it would be safer to employ professionals.

Two of our group had cars, one was an ex service man whose pre war car, a vintage open toped Bentley was brought out on special occasions, the other was an ex art student who had decided to become a doctor. His car was a very old MG. It was so old that its pointed tail was made of wood. The ancient red roadster stood out from the more modern cars. It's owner fondly likened it to a scrotum as it was a comfortable two seater. He wrote its name, 'scotum' on the side of the bonnet. Unfortunately, the police took a dim view of this and made him remove the name in case the term 'scotum' caused offence. This was after all the 1950s.

Hospital Life

I can well remember my first introduction to the hospital. Together with Roy and Garry, two of the ex-service contingent, we were assigned to the Casualty department. It was the forerunner of the present day accident and emergency units in the hospital. Patients with minor trauma, with lumps and bumps, too big to be treated in the GP's surgery, and the occasional workplace injury, were treated by junior medical staff under the watchful eye of the Resident Medical Officer (RMO)and Sister. After a brief introduction and a lesson on how to wash one's hands properly we were all given minor tasks to do. It fell to me to deal with an abscess in a patient's armpit, using what was described as the Hilton method (after the surgeon not the hotel). Roy, coming from a medical family was given a scalpel and instructed on how to remove an evil smelling sebaceous cyst, whilst Gary was told to remove the sutures from a patients arm. Having completed our tasks we assembled in sister's office for our reward of tea and biscuit, basking in the self satisfaction that comes with having saved another life. We sat around the office like obedient dogs that had obeyed his owner's orders and awaited our reward in the form of biscuits. Only Gary was not with us. I eventually found him in a treatment cubicle behind tightly drawn curtains. He was on the verge of tears and perspiring profusely whilst his victim, looking no less disconcerted, faced him with a look of abject terror. The six sutures on the arm remained intact but the skin around them was scratched, swollen and inflamed. Gary, discretely whispered his problem to me;-it appears no one had told him you have to cut the sutures in order to remove them; he had been trying to undo the knots.

The Medical Officer in charge of Casualty was a young married surgeon whose good looks were to prove a problem. He was in great demand as a male model and his image appeared regularly in the pages of fashion magazines. This was proving so lucrative that instead of using his spare time to study for his Fellowship examination he found the temptation of mammon so alluring that he took to skipping the tutorials in order to attend photo shoots. As a result it took him two or three attempts to pass his FRCS, the unavoidable hurdle to becoming a surgeon. Fearing his failure to sail through the examination would dog his path to fame he applied for a surgical post with the Colonial Office. To his delight they offered him a post as the surgeon to a colony in central Africa;- at last he could practice his surgical skills. Unfortunately after resigning his present post in preparation for the move to Africa he received a telephone call to tell him the incumbent surgeon had decided to do another tour of duty and the position would not now be open. It was suggested that he should 'come and see us, we may have something else for you'. He duly arrived and was ushered into the Chief's office where, having apologised for having to withdraw the offer of a post in Africa, the Chief told him that there was a general duties medical post available, that required the doctor to perform occasional surgical tasks. He was informed it was in a place called the Virgin Islands. When he enquired 'where were the Virgin Islands?' The Official from the Colonial Office was a bit vague but said he thought they were somewhere in the Pacific. When he enquired if there was any sailing there, as he was a keen yachtsman, the reply was 'I suppose so, after all its an island' That is how the future Captain of the Virgin Island Olympic sailing team came to settle in the island paradise of Tortola.

On the Wards

The Surgical Firm

After completing our introductory unit we were divided up into groups of six or seven and allocated either a medical or surgical firm. Now armed with our bright new stethoscopes and wearing our short white jackets, we became clerks on medical wards or dressers on surgical ones. Whilst on duty as a clerk we carried our ophthalmoscope, (as potent a symbol of being a physician as a stethoscope), in our bulging pockets. In truth, few of us ever managed to see anything of diagnostic importance with this compulsory, expensive bit of equipment but without it we felt we were not proper doctors.

Our week was spent taking the histories of new patients, following up their progress on the wards and attending out-patients and teaching rounds, As a dresser we would be expected to watch the great man demonstrating his surgical skills in the operating theatre and to laugh at his jokes or put downs. If the operation was upon a patient who had been assigned to us we were expected to scrub up with the surgical team so that we could stand immobile at the periphery of the field of action holding a retractor to expose the wound. Often this back breaking job would necessitate standing, with absolute rigidity, for several hours at a time. For this reason there was a premium in being assigned patients with only minor surgical conditions.

The dress code was rigidly enforced. Older consultants still arrived at the hospital in their formal black jackets with stripped trousers. Although wing collars had gone out of fashion, separate white collars secured by collar studs were always worn with a college, army unit or grey tie. Most consultants wore bowler hats outdoors. There was an occasion when one of the consultants was getting out of his car outside his club in Whitehall when he was spotted by two African girls, dressed in flowing, colourful robes. He was wearing his formal suit, guards tie and like all ex-guardsmen, he was wearing a bowler hat and carrying a tightly rolled umbrella. He stopped and posed for the girls as they took his photo. One can envisage that, back in Africa, they showed it to their friends as an example of 'a native in his habitat'

Only suits with white shirts and discrete ties were permissible on the wards. Beards were discouraged as a potential cess pits of bacteria. Our white coats had to be immaculate. When the great man set forth on his ward round a hush would fall over the ward. Bed clothes were straightened and the tops of the patient's lockers cleared of any clutter. Nurses, led by the ward sister, stood by ready to obey any of the great man's commands. It is impossible to know how these consultants would have fared today when patients, on admission to hospital, are given instructions on how to complain about their treatment and the names of solicitors who will make claims against the hospital and its staff on their behalf. There is no doubt that, at the time, the patient was expected to accept the decisions of the consultant without question. Today the expectation is that all patients should be informed about every detail of their treatment, the availability and success rate of alternative treatments, the comparative death and morbidity rates and the way to access the complaints procedure process. This has not improved the outcome of surgery but it has resulted in many more patients feeling disgruntled. One even complained that he had not been told that one of the surgical team looking after him was due to go on holiday.

Many ward rounds and outpatients that I recall became trials of strength between the Chief; the great man who presided over the proceedings attended by his fawning acolytes, and the students. This was particularly true of the ex-service men who saw the task of challenging authority as their inalienable right earned by years in the armed forces fighting the enemy. When on one ward round the surgeon asked his students the causes of his patient's wound failing to heal after the great man's surgical onslaught, back came the answer from one of the ex-service students-'bad surgery sir'. When anther surgeon insisted on wearing the red cotton in the button hole of his jacket, signifying that he had been awarded the Legion d'honeur, an ex service student took great delight in pointing out that he had left the cleaning tag in his suit jacket. When an ex-service registrar, who was assisting his chief at a difficult operation, found he was not able to see what the great man was doing as the table had been pumped up too high he asked a student nurse for a flat foot stool so that he could get a better view of the wound. His request was overheard by the surgeon who turned on him saying 'it must your flat feet that stops you from assisting me properly', to which the ex-serviceman, replied 'my feet weren't flat when we started this operation'!

One particularly enthusiastic surgeon insisted on operating all day on Saturdays and even on Christmas Eve. He was greeted on Christmas day with a streamer extending across the front of the hospital building proclaiming 'Surgeon X gives Green Shield Stamps'.

On those occasions when a patient was referred to a colleague for a second opinion, great care was taken in composing witty letters. One such patient, who complained that his penis became painfully bent when he achieved an erection, he was referred to the urologist with the words 'This man is on pleasure bent'. After his disease had been diagnosed he was sent back from the urologist with a letter saying 'I don't handle bent organs'.

The urologist was a witty surgeon and a good teacher but sometimes he was carried away by his own enthusiasm. There was one occasion when, attempting to demonstrate how a tumour of the thyroid gland in the neck could became so large that it distorted and displaced the wind pipe, he unwittingly pressed so hard on a poor student's trachea that he started to go blue and froth at the mouth. The other students thought he was faking his breathing difficulty until his knees began to buckle and he passed out

Neither the students nor the patients were a match for the quick wittedness of the staff. On one occasion an irate patient appeared at Sir Stanford Cade's outpatients and produced an envelop containing a large blood stained, evil smelling surgical swab, clearly imprinted 'Westminster Hospital'. After placing the swab on the table he turned accusingly to the surgeon saying 'this started to came out of my mouth whilst I was having my breakfast, it made me choke; it could have killed me'. Sir Stanford looked pityingly at the man who, started to slump in his seat. Stanford looked at the swab and turned his gaze back to his victim. He addressed the patient slowly and softly, like a mother admonishing a recalcitrant child, saying; 'you bloody fool. It was not meant to come out for another week'. The complainant visibly withered and stammered out his apology. It was an uneven battle between the great man and his patient.

There were occasions when the students were the butt of the great man's humour. When Roy was riffling through the patient's notes on a ward round, trying to find the results of a particular test, James Burn, his fellow dresser, quietly slipped away to try to find the missing laboratory sheet. His disappearance was quickly spotted by the great man who observed in a sonorous tone 'I see Roy fiddles whilst Burn roams'.

One particular surgical consultant had such a high opinion of his own unique ability to save lives that he was impossible to parody. On one occasion after telling a patient that he would cure her the next day by means of a very minor operation, the patient turned to the great man and said, sarcastically, 'in that case sir I will pray for God to guide your most talented hands' The great man, totally unabashed, looked at his hands, then, looking her in the eyes replied 'so you have noticed them'.

During his outpatients he insisted that all the students sat in a semi circle so as to catch every word he uttered. We were then made to write his wise sayings on what he termed, 'the constant battle against disease', in a little black book. I can recall the first entry, it was;- There are four requisites for a good surgeon, a good car (he of course had a Rolls Royce), a good secretary, a good light and a good wife- in that order my boy! It is said that his own marriage lasted less than two days. On one occasion when an Asian student came in late to his outpatient clinic he looked up and greeted him with the words, 'I see the news of my teaching has reached the Orient a little late'. During a formal award presentation he entered the auditorium dressed in the beautiful flowing red robes of an honorary Doctor of the University of

Bogotá declaiming, 'I am no ordinary surgeon, I am an International surgeon'. His wise words were not always without foundation, he would advise all those thinking of matrimony to first study the mothers of their intended wives so that the could look at what they might expect in the future. For all his pomposity he was a good teacher and his students still tell stories about the quotations in their little black books

Because many of the students and junior staff were older men, having served in the army, patients occasionally failed to realise who was the consultant and who the junior houseman. There was one notable occasion when the eminent consultant explained to the patient that he needed an operation on his lungs to 'straighten out a kink in his bronchial tubes' a euphemism for a cancerous growth in his lungs. To his consternation the patient replied that before he agreed to the operation, he would first have to consult Mr Y. The consultant was livid, Mr Y happened to be the great man's ex service junior house surgeon with less than six months experience as a doctor.

Assisting the surgeon in the operating theatre was an onerous duty. Too often you found yourself playing the part of a stooge in a variety act. Any complication or any error of judgement was always your fault. If your hand accidentally got in the great man's way it was likely to be hit with an instrument or there would be a threat that some awful complication was likely to be visited on the patient as a result of your incompetence. Unless you stood well back from the great man's field of vision it was likely that you would receive a kick on your shin or your head would be butted. You were constantly blamed for 'getting in the way of the light,'. On one occasion one of the ex-service students on being asked to assist a particular surgeon approached the operating table with the remark 'which light would you have me stand in front of, sir?' When a surgeon barked an order for an arm board to his ex serviceman dresser the student's was heard to mumble 'if he is bored how does he think the rest of us feel.' Fortunately it was said too softly for the surgeon to hear- he was left wondering why the rest of us fell about laughing.

Surgeons in those days prided themselves on the speed of their operations, it was a badge of honour, a sign of a superior dexterity. One surgeon took great delight in finishing his operation before the student, who had been sent to assist him, had finished scrubbing his hands and putting on his gown and gloves. He would feign mock surprise when the student presented himself just as the last stitch was going in.

I assisted at one operation, to repair a small congenital vascular defect near a baby's heart which was being performed as a demonstration before visiting dignitaries. In the time it took them to change from their suits into theatre garb the patient had been anaesthetised, the chest opened and the operation completed. They were in time to see the wound being dressed and the baby waking up.

Nevertheless, a lot of surgery was accomplished in a very competent fashion. The relationship, which was always tense during the operations, relaxed in the tea room once the list was completed and we sat around picking up words of advice and encouragement. It was after the surgeon left the field of battle that he once again became human. It was in these surroundings that the pose of 'captain of the ship' would be dropped and the post operative instructions would be discussed. It was then that the great man would reveal his concern for the well being of the patients on whom he had operated. It was then that one realised that they too were vulnerable. In later life, talking to the wives of some of these surgeons, one realised how often they would pace the floor throughout the night after a particularly difficult operation on a sick patient. There was one very austere paediatrician who was notorious for his exacting demands on ward rounds, who his wife assured me, was often in tears when one of his patients failed to survive surgery for the correction of a congenital heart defect.

The Medical Firm

There was considerably less drama on the medical wards. Physicians tended to cultivate the pose of 'learned gentry'. For example on the occasion when a student made a stupid remark, such as 'streptococci are gram negative bacteria', the consultant would gaze forgivingly at the unfortunate victim of and after a short period of apparent reflection might say, in a sarcastic tone, 'yes, you are right, a strain of gram negative streptococci was described by Prof Flugerman in 1922, it is good to find a student who is acquainted with his work'.

On one ward round a consultant geriatrician described how as one got older the ability to stand on one leg with one's eyes closed became impaired. In the Grapes public house that evening a group of us put this theory to the test. The younger students competed with the ex service students to see who could stand the longest, on one leg with his eyes closed. On opening our eyes we were surprised to find ourselves surrounded by a group of the regular drinkers who were speculating on whether we were taking part in an initiation rite into some weird new age cult or were undergoing mass hypnosis.

We were often given minor tasks to perform on the medical wards and soon became adept at taking blood, collecting urine specimens and occasionally performing a lumbar puncture. One of my colleagues had the misfortune to have his patient die within minutes of completing his first lumbar puncture. He took it as a sign from heaven. It was a long time before he recovered and he never again performed a lumbar puncture. To this day he maintains his record of achieving 100% mortality with his first and only surgical procedure.

Obstetrics

Not all our time was spent in the Teaching Hospital. For some firms we were rotated to St Stephen's Hospital in Fulham, now the site of the new Chelsea and Westminster Hospital. (It was to have been called the Westminster and Chelsea Hospital but some bright spark insisted if it were it would be known as the W.C. hospital).

In those days it was still an undisguised 'poor law' hospital. It had vast wards, echoing corridors, dark green institutional paint and unsanitary toilet and washing facilities. The atmosphere was totally different from the reverential overtones of the Teaching Hospital. The consultants were ordinary people who happened to be skilled and able doctors rather than the demi-gods of the teaching hospital. Even the consultants from Westminster Hospital who reluctantly agreed to attend the sick, on a part time basis, in these rather impoverished circumstance, dropped the pretence of intellectual superiority although they often gave the impression they were 'visiting relatives who had fallen on hard times'

For the students it was a relief, they could make mistakes without fear of being skewered by a barbed, cutting response from the great man, even the dress code was more casual although still strictly jacket and tie. It was true that some of the older consultants at the hospital were still wedded to techniques and treatment that we, raw students, had come to accept as old fashion and which provoked our disdain. The most positive side of this arrangement was that as students we became more focused on patient care rather than status, more orientated to the needs of the patient than the amore propre of the doctor.

It was at St Stephens Hospital that I had my introduction to the mysteries of childbirth. The hospital was also a maternity centre. Under the watchful eye of Sister Anne Marie Magee, I learnt how a baby was born and how not to make the process any harder or more painful than necessary. Sister Magee was a good teacher and was adept at dealing with what to some of us was an embarrassing experience. She would stand no nonsense and did not tolerate fools readily. On hearing herself referred to as Sister amenorrhea Magee, she retaliated by using expressed breast milk instead of cow's milk in our tea. It is a taste that only new born babies can get to like. As a result of her instruction and the indulgence of those giving birth at the hospital, I became sufficiently skilled in midwifery to be permitted to return to Westminster to do my stint 'on the district.

On The District

Being 'on the district' provided the first taste of what it was like to be a proper doctor. Although one was, in theory, attached to an experienced midwife in practice it did not always work out as planned, due to the contingencies of the service and the inability to persuade the mothers not to 'pop' their babies, all at the same time.

We were provided with a room in the hospital so that we could be readily available and 'on call'. It was designated as a bedroom but there was no toilet or washing facilities and the bed linen was only changed when someone remembered. Immediately outside the door was the communal wash basin which was used by the midwives to wash their instruments after a delivery and by the student in the mornings. It was not unusual to emerge from the room to find one's way impeded by piles of blood soaked linen and soiled towels and the only wash basin being used as an instrument laundry. There was inevitable friction between the midwives and the students which was not helped by the students ruse of emerging from their rooms stark naked in the expectation that the midwives would flee the field of battle leaving them masters of the wash basin. As a result the relationship between the district midwives and students became like that in an undeclared war.

Looking back, I think my time on the district was the scariest time I ever experienced in medicine.

On one occasion I arrived at a tiny flat in a run down Peabody Estate for the delivery of a first baby to a blind physiotherapist. She had been blinded at birth when the wrong drops were put in her eyes in a provincial hospital. As a result she was terrified of having her baby in any hospital. When I arrived I was told that the midwife was delayed and 'please could I get everything ready'. The delivery bed was a very low divan, which meant that I would have to lie down flat on the floor to control the birth of the baby. The light was a single overhead 60 watt bulb which failed to illuminate the area of the prospective battle. I persuaded the mother- to- be to lie down on the divan whilst I sorted out the instruments. Too my horror she started having strong labour pains almost at once. I rapidly rearranged the instruments, gowned and gloved up and started to clean the patient's bottom with the antiseptic with which I had been provided. It was at this moment that the huge guide dog burst into the room. It had smelt the alcohol in the antiseptic on the patient's bottom and proceeded to start licking the mother-to-be's perineum. As I had a prepared myself for the delivery by putting on a sterile gown and gloves, my ability to tackle the animal was severely limited. All I could do was to try to kick out to try to shy it away. The dog must have misinterpreted my efforts as an attack on his mistress. He started to growl then to tear at my trouser and bite my leg. In desperation I threw an alcohol swab at the dog but the intense cold that was caused by the evaporation of the alcohol only intensified the dog's aggression. He bared his teeth and bit my leg. I felt the trickle of blood oozing from the wound. In the ensuing tussle all pretence at anti septic practice was lost. It became a fight for survival between me and the dog.

Fortunately, being the first baby, the labour was fairly prolonged and just as the baby's head started to appear, the midwife turned up. The baby was gigantic and whilst I wrestled with the dog the midwife took over the delivery. It was chaos. The dog would not let go, the growling became louder; the midwife had to make a large cut to allow the head to escape. There was blood everywhere and to my dismay, some of it was mine. Eventually the dog was removed, the door secured and the 10lb baby delivered. It proved impossible to sew up the tear in the mother's bottom properly whilst she was lying on the divan and I had to lie on the floor in an attempt to control the bleeding wound. In the end I settled for a few big sutures to control the bleeding and decided the repair would have to be done at a later date when we could operate in better conditions at the hospital.

I was too preoccupied during my battle with the dog to even enquire as to the baby's sex. I fled the scene as soon as the midwife had taken control, with a large dressing on my bleeding leg. I never discovered what the poor blind mother thought about the goings on. I decided it was prudent to absent myself when she presented at the hospital for a definitive repair of the wound in her perineum.

I was not the only student to meet difficulties. One of my fellow students was congratulating himself (as well as the mother) after the baby was born and it lay between the mother's legs, with the umbilical cord still attached, when suddenly the mother gave a scream and cried out that she had a dreadful cramp in her leg. The pain caused her to kick out. Unfortunately her leg caught the baby which shot away still attached to the elastic umbilical cord. My friend responded brilliantly, he performed a rugby tackle and saved the baby from hitting the wall.

As the baby was catapulted forward the umbilical cord became stretched like a bow string until finally it detached the placenta from inside the mother's uterus. Once free, the placenta rocketed out with great force and hit him squarely in the face with a resounding splash.

I am sure that there are many normal, happy uneventful deliveries carried out 'on the district' unfortunately I seemed to have missed them!

The Eye Firm

There were other special firms covering subjects such as eye disease, skins and anaesthetics which had to be completed before we were allowed to sit for the qualifying examinations.

The eye unit was run by a charismatic surgeon whose brother was a prominent Oxford don whose activities in the service of MI6 were generally well known. Unfortunately he was extremely absent minded and would often turn up an hour late for the teaching round. On one occasion, after putting drops into a patient's eyes in the dark room, he totally forgot about her. She was left trying to find the way out of the blacked out dark room whilst virtually blinded by the effect of the eye drops. A cleaner eventually heard her cries coming from the room some three hours later and released her from captivity. Another time, during a teaching round, he told the six of us to follow him to see an interesting patient; absent mindedly he popped into the toilet on the way to the ward oblivious of the embarrassment caused to the female student, who like the rest of us, had followed his instruction and followed him into the men's toilet.

The Anaesthetic Firm

We were required to be 'signed up' for having given ten anaesthetics under supervision. I was so put off by my first experience that I persuaded one of the anaesthetic registrars to complete the list of signatures in return for a pint of beer in the bar.

The trouble had started when my instructor suggested I should first learn how to give an ether anaesthetic before progressing to more modern methods that involved injecting poisons into patients. My instructor turned out to be Sir Ivan Magill, a delightful leprechaun from Belfast. It was Magill who had introduced endotracheal intubation into common practice when he was required to anaesthetise patients with severe facial burns and injuries, during the 1914-18 war.

He presented me with a gauze covered face mask and a bottle of ether which he told me to drip slowly onto the mask until the patient went to sleep. At least that was the theory; in practice it caused the patient to start coughing, gagging, vomiting and fighting to remove the mask from his face. In the process he wet himself, sat up on the trolley and he was squaring up to hit me, when Magill took over. He showed me how it should be done. He picked up his bottle dripped the contents onto a new mask (the first still contained bile stained vomit), and slowly but sweetly the patient went quietly to sleep. The difference between his administration and my own was remarkable. It was only years later that I discovered the old rogue's bottle contained chloroform with just enough ether to cover the smell of chloroform. There is a world of difference between the ease with which the pungent, irritating ether can be administered and that of the potent non-irritating chloroform.

The Refresher Course

As the time for the examinations approached we were given tutorials and mock vivas to prepare us for the battle ahead. Amongst the tutors was a young surgeon from Oxford who turned out to be a brilliant undergraduate lecturer. Harold Ellis eventually went on to become the first professor of surgery at Westminster Hospital. Harold had published a seminal paper in the BMJ describing a new type of injury caused by the recently introduced zip fastening on the fly of the trousers issued to US soldiers. In the paper he described the repair of a zip injury to the foreskin of American soldier.

Our therapeutics revision sessions were taken by a no nonsense Yorkshireman. His favourite put down, when one of the students had suggested a less than effective remedy, was 'you might as well give them buffalo's urine'. It was not long before this became a catch phrase describing any of the many useless treatments.

The revision course meant giving up even the occasional visit to the local curry house or the pub; the library and the museum became our home. Fewer and fewer sorties were made into the nearby nurses home to seek solace and comfort from the creatures of mercy who lived there. Nevertheless, students being what they are there were the occasional opportunities to have fun.

It was on April 1st, all fools day, that three unfortunate GPO workman appeared outside the Medical School to start working on the road for repairs to the underground telephone wires. They had no sooner set up the barriers, assembled their tools and their little canvas hut with its GPO logo, and settled down to their first cup of tea, when they were furtively approached by one of the students. He whispered to them that he had heard his colleagues in the bar plotting an April Fools' day prank. He explained they were going to dress up as policemen and come and ask them to show their permits and details of the instructions for their work in order to object to the obstruction they were causing to the footpath. Whilst this was taking place his fellow plotters telephoned the local police station to explain that a group of students had found a GPO canvas hut and had 'borrowed' it. They had dressed up as workmen and they were going to start obstructing the road outside the Medical School. Once the plot was hatched, all the students had to do was to sit back and enjoy the resulting scene from the safety of the Medical School bar. The police thought the workman phoney and the workman believed the police-men to be students. It took them about an hour to sort it out and to realise that it was all an April Fools' day joke. It caused another official deputation of complaint to the Dean who had watched the episode unfold from the windows of his office, thoroughly enjoying the prank.

There was inevitably a considerable amount of fraterni-sation between the nurses and the students, relationships that might start during spells of duty on the wards or when seeking some inside information about a patient that one might use to score an advantage on the ward rounds. These might blossom if there was a 'hop' in the nurse' home or a student party. From time to time there was a scandal when a nurse's belt or cloak was found in a student's room whilst he was living in 'on the house'. Invariably the nurse would be reported to Matron and sacked on the spot. It was up to Matron to uphold the chaste image of nursing just it was regarded as manly for a medical students to try to encourage a nurse into his bed. Most of these relationships were short lived but some continued after qualification. Many happy marriages started in this manner.

The Finals

The examinations were soon upon us. The exam was in four parts and one had to pass every part to qualify. The pass rate was fairly high, in the region of 75%, so statistically one had to be unlucky or idle to fail a part of the test but as one had to pass all parts to qualify as a doctor the possibility of failure was greatly increased. If many examinees failed just one part, there would be a large cull of students and less competition for the precious 'house jobs'. It was the viva voce examinations that were particularly unpredictable. Held in the hallowed Victorian Examination halls in Queen's Square one prayed to be allocated a co-operative or helpful patient to examine in order to make a sensible diagnosis. During the breaks for coffee and tea the students would gather in the garden of the square to compare notes about their terrifying experiences with this or that examiner. Most patients were very sympathetic to the plight of the nervous students who confronted them and questioned them about their symptoms and habits. It was not unknown for them to tell the anxious student 'I've got this disease', or 'your supposed to listen to my chest just here'. The worst patients were children who very often appeared to have nothing wrong with them and who answered each questions, such as 'are you short of breathe with 'spose I am'. I was confronted with one such obnoxious child whose only present abnormality was having egg shell blue coloured 'whites' to his eyes, a sign pathognomic of a rare congenital disease. I examined him carefully but could find nothing wrong except that he was short for his age. He answered all my enquiries as though we were playing a game of 20 questions. Each question would be answered with a grudging monosyllabic 'yes' or 'no' or 'perhaps'. He obviously regarded the examination as a personal challenge in which he would give away as little as possible. I became increasingly desperate. I examined every part of his body minutely. As the allocated time ticked by I was in a panic. It was only at the last minute, when he started openly laughing-he had won, that I noticed the odd colour of the whites of his eyes.

At last the examinations were over. We could put down our text books, have a great party and go on holiday. The relief came as a shock, there was suddenly a void in one's life. There was nothing further to be done until the results were announced. The results of these examinations were tremendously important, to fail your finals was, in the intensively competitive world of post war medicine, like loosing at a game of Russian roulette. Obtaining an all important 'first house job', on which one's future hung, depended upon achieving a good result in the finals examinations.

Chapter Four

The House Jobs

I was in Torquay, on holiday, when the results of the qualifying examinations came out. I could not face the humiliation of a failure so I funked visiting the hospital and took my first real holiday for three years. I was haunted by the thought that I had imagined the pale blue colour of the 'whites' of the eyes of the child who had tormented me in the medicine viva. In the event I had no reason to be terrified-I had passed. Even better, I had secured a coveted 'honours' in pharmacology and therapeutics. As one of the two students who had achieved an honours pass, I was assured of one of the good house jobs at my hospital. There were four prime jobs. Two in medicine and two in surgery. With my fellow newly qualified doctors, I spent the next few days canvassing the support of the consultants who would be my chiefs, were I to be selected. I waited expectantly for the day when the result of the selection process was announced. To my utter dismay when they were posted I found I had been appointed to be house physician to the Gordon Hospital, the annexe in Vincent Square noted, not for its medical practice, but for its surgery. By a strange co-incidence the hospital was built on the site of the nursing home where I had been born some 25 years earlier.

The Gordon Hospital had a distinguished surgical staff and it acted as the gastro intestinal unit of Westminster Hospital. It was there that the pioneering method of removing cancer of the rectum, by what was called the synchronous combined abdomino-perineal resection, was introduced by Ernest Miles. It had a medical unit but for the most part the unit provided post operative care for any surgical patient who became desperately ill after their operations. Today, most of those patients would be looked after in a Recovery or Intensive Care Unit.

I went to the local pub with several other disconsolate fellow students who had also failed to obtain the house jobs they had wanted. It became a fairly noisy affair and with the help of several pints of beer and the enthusiastic banter of the newly qualified doctors, my depression was beginning to lift when a consultant anaesthetist I recognised tapped me on the shoulder and took me into one corner. He explained that he was in charge of anaesthetics at the Gordon Hospital and that it was due to his intervention that I had been given the post of house physician at the Gordon. He said it was a golden opportunity as there were not a lot of medical beds and I would be able to help him out with the anaesthetic duties. As a person with my background in physiology and pharmacology, he explained, I should pick up the principals of anaesthesia very quickly and enjoy the experience. Had I not been under the effects of too much alcohol, too dejected by my failure to get the house post I coveted and less in awe of my superiors; I would have hit him! All I could think about was my miserable experience whilst trying to put someone to sleep by dropping ether onto a mask on a patient's face. Visions of the half crazed man sitting up on the operating trolley about to punch me came to mind. The thought of going through that sort of experience every day was more than I could bear. It was as if someone was rubbing the salt of ignominy into the wound caused by the rejection of my application for a post at the main hospital. In the event all I could bring myself to say was 'thank you sir'.

That is how, on September the first 1955, I reported for duty as the house physician to the Gordon Hospital. My immediate boss was the highly respected, senior physician to St. Bartholomew's Hospital, Dr. Edward. Cullinan.

House Physician

The consultant anaesthetist who was responsible for my appointment was correct, there were only about six regular medical beds at the Gordon Hospital and most of them were occupied by long termed patients with chronic stomach complaints. In those days, a month stay in hospital, hoping that nature would cure the prob-lem before the medical treatment made it worse, was common. In all my time as a house physician I cannot remember a patient, in whom the primitive remedies we provided seemed to make a significant difference to the eventual outcome of their disease. On the other hand patients passed through the surgical wards much more rapidly, usually greatly relieved or cured. I think it was this experience that determined me, at that time, to become a surgeon.

If the ward work was light, the out patients was busy and hard work. This was a gastro intestinal unit at a time when gastric ulcers and stress disorders of the bowels were common. Dr Cullinan had a particular reputation with the Polish émigré community in London and they constituted a high proportion of our patients. Most showed evidence of depression and stress. We came to recognise a particular Polish syndrome known as the 'Umptere syndrome'. The patient would point to his stomach and complain of pain 'ere', then moving his finger to his groin saying 'umptere' then on to his elbow, umptere and so on until any attempt at taking a meaningful history became futile. All one could do was to rule out serious pathology and reassure the patients. Many seemed to benefit from having an X ray or an ECG. In fact one old lady insisted the ECG had done her so much good 'could she please have a course of them!' As I came towards the last months of my house post I started to give a follow up date for the umpteres to co-incide with the first outpatient clinic of my successor. I am told he had a succession of eight such patients to deal with when he took his first clinic;-he later told me he was about to resign his post there and then when he was placated and told that this clinic had been stage managed.

Dr Cullinan was a considerate chief. He had recently bought the ruined light house on Beachy Head. It had been used for target practice during the war. He made a habit of inviting his housemen to his home in Sussex, for a day in the country. He explained we should dress informally. What he did not tell us until we arrived was that we were expected to help rebuild the stone work that had been shattered by the shelling during the war. In all fairness, after several hours of back breaking labour he usually provided a splendid meal.

Life at the Gordon

As the consultant anaesthetist had predicted I spent much of my time giving anaesthetics and supervising post-operative recovery problems. These often presented testing medical challenges that responded rapidly to active medical intervention. It was here one saw sick patients getting better as a result of one's treatment. This was why I had become a doctor, at last I could see I was doing good.

It is difficult today to appreciate the rapid transition that new doctors had to make, from medical student to a practitioner, as soon as they qualified. Today the transition period is managed more carefully but in those days you were either an ignorant student or a qualified doctor. So it was, some three weeks after starting work as a doctor, I received a telephone call from a well known consultant anaesthetist to say he was held up (he anaesthetised at another hospital for Dickson Wright who was a notoriously bad time keeper) and could I please do his case for him. I looked on the operation list and found he was due to anaesthetise for the senior surgeon to perform a major abdominal cancer operation in fifteen minutes time. I told him I had never anaesthetised anyone unsupervised before, to which he replied 'its easy, just slip in a spinal'. After consulting the books and learning rapidly about such mysteries as hyperbaric solutions, barbotage and isobaric techniques I decided if nurses and technicians could do it so could I, after all, I was a proper doctor. To my horror I then discovered the patient, was a private patient and as such he presumed he was buying the very best treatment available-well, he was getting me so I had better act as though I knew what I was doing. In fact all went so well that the surgeon thanked me profusely and the anaesthetist, who was able to bill the patient for my services, gave me my first private fee of 10 guineas. At last I really was a proper doctor. I had to decide whether to use the fee to celebrate or to frame it. Never one for avoiding the inevitable, the fee was spent on a curry dinner for the resident doctors at the hospital

Life at the Gordon soon settled down into a routine. The consultant anaesthetist who had earmarked me for his assistant became a valued friend and adviser. His operating lists were almost always in the mornings. They would be followed by a sandwich lunch at the nearby Surprise public house, accompanied by a pint of beer. We would then settle down to have a doze until 3.00pm when I would start the afternoon registrar list, whilst he listened to the sport or racing, on the radio. The list would often not finish until 6.30pm leaving time for a quick ward round, to make sure all was well with the patients, before dinner in the mess at 7.30 pm.

On one occasion, shortly after I started working at the Gordon, I arrived early in the operating suite to find a man dressed in a suit taking all the black rubber corrugated tubing off the anaesthetic machine and immersing it in a bucket of water. I was mystified by this strange behaviour especially as I had no idea who he was. I tackled the interloper aggressively asking him 'what the hell he thought he was doing'. It turned out he was an occasional anaesthetist who, some months previously had been giving an anaesthetic at another hospital when the cyclopropane anaesthetic gas in the anaesthetic circuit exploded due to static electricity generated in the very dry atmosphere He said he would not now give an anaesthetic without first soaking all the rubber tubing. I was reminded of this event when, some years later, I watched an anaesthetist, at another hospital,using the same explosive anaesthetic, cyclopropane, at the head of the table whilst the surgeon performed a cystoscopy on the patient's bladder at the other end of the operating table, gowned and gloved whilst smoking a cigar!

Whilst I was the house physician at the Gordon Hospital one of the consultant surgeons decided to try out a new operation for the treatment of gastric ulcers. Although the objective of the operation was based on the current belief that the ulcers were due to too much gastric acidity, a belief we now know to be only partly true, the operation had never been tested in animals. At that time a new untried treatment could be carried out at the behest of the consultant without permission of his peers or any scrutiny by an ethics committee. Although it was the usual practice to tell the patient that you were trying out a new treatment there was no obligation to inform the patient and patient consent was not considered to be necessary. The consultant accepted total responsibility for any treatment that he, or his juniors, carried out. He knew that if anything went wrong, he carried the can. In this particular case the operation was a failure and resulted in all the victims being subjected to another major procedure to undo the first operation. Had we known more about the cause of stomach ulcers at the time, it would have been known to be pointless. Within a short time the ulcer invariably re-occurred necessitating a lengthy operating session to reverse the original procedure. This was a complicated affair as it resulted in having to join together five cut ends of bowel to make two continuous ones.

How different from present day practice. Although undoubtedly well intentioned the practice was indefensible. We told ourselves that the patients never suffered but having unnecessary operations, was indeed subjecting patients to an avoidable risk and pain. To do so without the patient appreciating what was happening could never be justified. Not being obliged to discuss the proposed experimental technique with independent, informed colleagues resulted in some bizarre procedures being carried out, from time to time, in the name of research. On one occasion I was called upon to anaesthetise a patient who had been pronounced dead from a cardiac infarct. The consultant surgeon had the strange idea that if he could get his heart working again by restoring its coronary circulation by surgery the patient would somehow come back to life. I shudder to think what would have happened had this Lazarus operation worked and the dead brought back to life.

It was always wrong, to put too much power into the hands of the researcher however well intentioned their efforts. Today, the process has swung to the opposite extreme. Any procedure, however minor and risk free, requires the approval of an Ethics Committee. Too often their decisions have nothing to do with ethics or morality but is a means of protecting the hospital from unnecessary expense and the risk of being sued should any patient feel they have been mistreated. It has become a way of delaying the majority of clinical investigations until the opportunity to carry them out has passed. It has resulted in the virtual extinction of clinical research-research that is the seed corn of major advances in medicine.

The Gordon Hospital was a sociable place, well known for its parties. At least one house surgeon was obliged to depart before the end of his six months appointment because of his amours with a physiotherapist. This was particularly embarrassing as he happened to be a nephew of one of the consultants. Not infrequently, after a party, a group of us would pile into cars and head for Heathrow airport or Covent garden market where, at that time, the bars remained open all night. We always had to make certain that our patients were left well supervised before we left the hospital. I was in a fortunate position as I seldom had any really sick patients. As a result it was not difficult to get another houseman to stay on call for my two or three patients. After these parties it was our usual practice to postpone the start of the following day's operating list so that doctors and nurses could sleep late and have time to recover from the exertions of the previous night. As the timing of the operating lists was always subject to negotiation between the resident registrar and the senior theatre nurse, who was always invited to the parties, this was seldom a problem.

Today, our behaviour would result in us being sacked and possibly being up before the GMC. It certainly would not be tolerated by the present hospital management. In defence of those times there is no doubt that it resulted in the development of a tremendous corporate spirit. We were a tight knit community supporting each other. Our first duty was always the welfare of our patient and this was never compromised. Our patients always received the best treatment that we could offer. The huge benefit to the housemen was that they learnt many practical skills quickly from the registrars and nurses. It allowed them rapidly to cross the divide between an unsure student and a competent doctor. Most evenings we would end up in the nurses rest room next to the operating theatre having coffee and biscuits with the duty staff. In those days, before the advent of disposable gloves and syringes, the nurses would spend the evenings sharpening syringe needles, lubricating glass syringes and repairing punctured rubber gloves. During these sessions we would exchange information about the patients in the hospital who were causing anxiety and about the following day's operations. All of us became involved in the progress of all the sick patients in the hospital. We became completely submerged in an atmosphere of medicine and patient care. Medicine became a way of life not just another job. It left little room for a family life or for any other activity.

There was one occasion that caused me considerable anxiety during this time. It resulted in a quick telephone call to the Medical Defence Union. It happened some five weeks after I had started my house job. I was giving an anaesthetic to a patient who was having his piles surgically excised. It was customary in those times to place the patient on his side on the operating table before putting him to sleep as this meant that the porter could be relieved to fetch another patient from the ward. I inserted a needle into his forearm, as usual and injected the then standard, high concentration of pentothal to put him to

sleep. To my dismay he took a long time becoming anaesthetised; this made me suspicious. It was when a patchy
red wheal appeared over the forearm that the penny
dropped. I realised that instead of injecting the drug into
a vein I had given it into an 'aberrant' artery (this is present in about 5% of patients). Several cases of this type of
accident had been reported in the anaesthetic literature
and I knew it carried a risk to the skin and muscles of his
hand. It was recommended that a dose of anticoagulant,
such as heparin, should be given to reduce the risk of
thrombosis. Unfortunately the surgery was underway
and there was little point in stopping it at this stage. After
a discussion with the consultant in the next theatre I gave
the heparin in spite of the increased risk of bleeding from
the wound and kept my fingers crossed. As soon as
I could, I telephoned the Medical Defence Union and
received advice that would be considered unethical
today. I was told to tell the patient that he had been 'aller-
gic' to the anaesthetic; under no circumstances should I
tell him the truth. The patient's arm did become quite
swollen and the fingers a little blue. After talking to the
other doctors in the mess I was advised to elevate his hand
by hanging it from a drip stand. I visited the patient two
or three times every day after the accident. I all but tucked
him up at nights. After four days the swelling had gone
down and his fingers were substantially normal-I could
breathe again. When at the end of the week the patient
left the hospital he left me a £5 present in gratitude for
the fantastic attention and care he had received! Another
curry celebration was called for.

At the end of my six months as a House Physician I was
undecided about my future. I had enjoyed the challenge

of providing anaesthesia but I hankered after the fame and kudos of the surgeon. I wanted to be the Captain of my Ship. Good surgical house posts were difficult to come by but fortunately my consultant anaesthetist friend at the Gordon had served in the army with a surgeon at one of the most famous surgical units in London. Such was the strong community spirit that had developed amongst us during the past six months that he volunteered to telephone his colleague and persuade him that I was just the person he needed as his house surgeon. It says a lot for his powers of persuasion that I was the first house surgeon that they appointed who had not yet obtained the first part of his surgical fellowship examination. So it was that I joined the distinguished band of junior doctors at the Royal Northern Hospital in the Holloway Road in London.

House Surgeon

The Royal Northern Hospital was a large Victorian building with a 1930's annexe that housed the Private, St David's Wing. It is the only hospital I have worked in where a ward round was literally just that. The wards were round. This was disconcerting as one often forgot at whose bed one had started and found oneself taking a history from a patient for a second time as one unwittingly started on a second lap of the ward.

The doctor's accommodation was primitive but clean. We soon became used to the cockroaches in our bedrooms and corridors and invented ingenious ways of racing them in cockroach Derbys. Telephones had not yet been installed in the resident's rooms. This was some time before the introduction of bleepers. After we had retired to our beds we were called from our rooms by messengers stationed in the porter's lodge. This curtailed the amorous pursuits of some of my colleagues. There was no library for the residents but there was a large mess for all the staff. Invariably there was a continuous game of bridge being played in one of the corners. Everyone played bridge and as soon as one doctor was called away to deal with an emergency, another would pick up his hand. These games usually did not end until well after midnight.

Although not an undergraduate teaching hospital The Royal Northern Hospital ran a heavily oversubscribed fellowship course for aspiring surgeons from around the world. It was renowned for its teaching having trained many famous surgeons. Its surgical reputation owed much to two surgeons, Hamilton Bailey and McNeil Love. These two surgical teachers had produced the world's best selling text books of surgery. They were the bible of every aspiring surgeon. They also produced several beautifully illustrated surgical manuals. Hamilton Bailey had undoubtedly been the driving force behind the teaching programme. Unfortunately he had died a few years before I arrived at the hospital. It is told that he had an unfortunate experience whilst watching his son arriving, at a London train terminus, from boarding school in the country. Sadly, the boy had lent out of the window as the train approached the station. It is told that Hamilton Bailey looked on as his son's head was smashed by a post as the train pulled into the platform. Following this tragic incident he became a recluse. I saw several of his follow-up patients in my clinic. The one I still remember had the longest surgical scar I have ever seen. He had performed a left side mastectomy and appendectomy on the patient through the same enormous incision. It started over the point of her left shoulder and continued down to her right groin.

Amongst the other surgeons was Reginald Murley (who became President of the Royal College of Surgeons and was duly knighted) and Mr Gabriel, who, because he was a famous as a specialist rectal surgeon, was known as 'the arse angel Gabriel'. In all there were four general surgeons, a urological surgeon and two ear nose and throat surgeons. Looking back at those times, I am sure that one of the reasons that the hospital was able to achieve such a distinguished staff was the presence of the adjacent private patient wing. This allowed it to attract distinguished surgeons who could supplement their income from the NHS by operating upon private patients in the adjoining building.

I was to be the house surgeon to McNeil Love, Reginald Murley and Mr Alex Roche, the urological surgeon. Of the four housemen, three of us ended up as Professors in different branches of medicine.

All three consultant surgeons had their individual eccentricities. The urological surgeon, Alex Roche, wrote humorous poetry and was much given to proclaiming Shakespearian soliloquies during his operations. His favourite 'first act' would take place as he approached a freshly prepared abdomen laid out on the operating table like an offering to the Gods. He would pick up a scalpel and, holding it like a dagger in his right hand, lunge at the abdomen with the words 'as he plucked forth his accursed steel note how the blood of Caesar flowed'. He would seldom be disappointed at the gush of blood that followed his first cut!

Before he started his out-patients session he would send for the large calendar that adorned the wall and count off the number of sessions until he retired. Although his surgical results were good and he had a very low rate of complications, he was stuck with many out of date surgical practices. His favourite aphorisms were; 'get them good and infected' and 'a little infection was good for healing'. As many of our urological patients were elderly with chronic urinary tract infections and strictures due to burnt out venereal disease, his disdain for using antibiotics too freely, was probably wise. Sadly, he died within six months of his retirement.

Gabriel was a very tall distinguished man with a military bearing. On one occasion when I had to call him back to the hospital in the middle of the night to tend a private patient who was bleeding, he arrived at 1.30 in the morning in his pin stripped trousers and black jacket which was adorned with a carnation. Being a top surgeon meant that standards had to kept up even in the dead of night. Today the consultant would be wearing jeans and a T-shirt!

I first met McNeil Love the day after I started my job as his house surgeon. He was still something of a legend although, at the time, he was approaching retirement. He was much less formal than the 'great men' who were the surgical adornments of the teaching hospitals. His repu-tation as a teacher brought students to watch him oper-ate from all parts of the world. We met by arrangement in the Private Wing coffee room. The first question he put to me seemed weird, it was 'is there anything in the freezer for me?'. Seeing my look of bewilderment he repeated his request in a more direct way; 'has any private patient left any money for me?' These were the days before medical insurance and most patients paid in cash for their operations.

Once that problem was sorted out we got along well. Our first outpatient session was business like with the registrar and me seeing the routine patients and McNeil Love teaching a group of about 15 post graduates on the more unusual cases. At the end of the session we made up the operating list for the following day. McNeil Love said he would operate on the three major cases leaving the three minor ones for myself and the registrar. The first of these was a bilateral hernia repair. He suggested that I should do one side and, at the same time, the registrar should repair the other side. In that way we could finish the list at a reasonable hour. The problem for me was that I had never performed more than a very minor operation before and although I had seen hernias being repaired I had never actually done one. Still there had to be a first time especially if I was to become a surgeon.

I prided myself that I knew the anatomy of the region well and that my dissecting skills were up to the task. So it was, towards the end of the Tuesday afternoon operating list that I was a confronted with my first real challenge as a surgeon. With a nurse to assist me I incised the patient's abdomen, exposed the hernial sac and displayed the margins of the muscular defect. By this time the registrar was starting to repair his side of the abdomen. As instructed, I tied off the sac and watched it disappear into the abdominal cavity. So far so good. I used strong catgut sutures to bring the edges of the muscle together; this was rather more difficult than I had realised as the muscle was very worn out and thin. I darned the defect with a running suture and closed the wound in the classical fashion. I had performed my first operation without a problem and, although somewhat slower than the registrar, it was carried out in good time. I was congratulating myself as the nurse applied the dressing whilst the anaesthetist lightened the anaesthesia and took the endotracheal tube from out of the patient's mouth. The patient gave a little twitch as he woke up, followed by an explosive cough. As I stood there watching the patient I saw an ominous bulge appear under the newly applied dressing over my hernia repair; slowly it grew larger and larger. It became increasingly obvious that my repair was giving way as the patient went into a paroxysm of coughing. Although about 10% of all hernia repairs fail, mine must have set an all time record for the most rapid recurrence!

Although I continued to carry out a weekly operation session, operating on such minor surgical problems as varicose veins, lumps and sebaceous cysts, I found my enthusiasm for surgery diminishing. Whether it was my unfortunate experience with my first hernia repair or the repetitive nature of much of the cutting and sewing it is difficult to tell. Certainly, it held little of the glory and fame associated with the great man in the teaching hospital. I enjoyed making a diagnosis and discussing the most suitable treatments for the patients that presented in the out patient's department or in the casualty but the actual surgery itself did not give me the same buzz that other keener types seemed to enjoy. To them surgery was a thrill,

like an actor performing on a stage. To me it was reduced
to a technical feat, more akin to dressmaking! Indeed,
some years later I expressed this view in a spoof article
written for the satirical medical magazine, World Medicine. Under the title of 'Need surgeons be Medically Qualified' I suggested that aspiring surgeons took a diploma in
knitting and sewing, the FRCS, Fellowship of the Royal
College of Seamstresses. The cover of the journal bore a
picture of a butcher performing petit point tapestry while
surrounded by scalpels and medical swabs. It made me
few friends amongst the surgeons, especially when it was
syndicated and reported in many papers around the
world. It was translated into seven languages where it was
presented as a serious proposition. The final straw came
when our Professor of Surgery received a letter from India
saying that the writer was a talented seamstress, very good
at needlework and petit point and could she please come
to England to do surgery in his unit?

As time went on I decided that I would not make a good
surgeon. Not only did I find the surgeon's emphasis on
technique and technical, manual skills unattractive but I
decided I could not tie knots; an essential requisite of a
good surgeon. I did not want to be a technician, cutting
and sewing, taking out lumps and bumps or joining tubes,
such as bowel or blood vessels, together. I was trained as
a scientist and it was this aspect of medicine that I found
most appealing. It is not that surgeons are any less well
informed than others in the profession. Most of the
ones I have worked with were excellent doctors, it is that
I felt surgery should be the last resort, an admission that
we could not cure the patient in any other way, rather
than an answer to a medical problem. I could not share

the enthusiasm of my surgical colleagues which centered around their displays of technical dexterity.

It was an occasion in one outpatient clinic that finally made me decide that I would not make a good surgeon. McNeil Love had been teaching on a young Cypriot lady with a large swelling behind her knee. He had asked the students to describe the lump, its size, its consistency and its edges. They concluded it was a large fatty swelling, a lipoma. I examined the lump and was quite certain it was fluid filled because it trans-illuminated; that is if you put a lighted torch to one side the whole cyst glowed. I quietly mentioned this to McNeil Love who dismissed it as irrelevant. He told me 'It's a lipoma, you can remove it in one of your sessions'. In due course the lady appeared on my operating list. She was anaesthetised and placed face down on the operating table. As I carefully cut down on the lump it soon became apparent it was, as I had predicted, a large fluid filled cyst. I had never seen anything like it before but from the little balls of material floating inside it I recognised it as a hydatid cyst. I had only seen this sort of thing before in a bottle in a museum. It is caused by tape worm infestation. These cysts are very rare in the UK but are endemic in some farming communities, especially where there is close contact between sheep, or woolly dogs, and man. After consulting the text books of surgery as to what should be done, I excised the cyst and irrigated the wound with formalin to kill any daughter cysts.

I described the case as a patient with a hydatid cyst in the popliteal fossa at the following Saturday morning Grand Teaching round. I pointed out that we had diagnosed the lump as a lipoma and were unprepared to find it was a cyst. I was put on the spot when a rather cocky post graduate student tried to score a point by asking loudly why we had not elicited a 'hydatid thrill'. This sign is typical of a fluid sac and is evoked by taping one side of a swelling and noting the pressure wave, or thrill, as it crosses the fluid filled sac. I could hardly explain that my chief, the great McNeil Love, had insisted that the lump was solid fat or that I had pointed out it transilluminated. Fortunately, Reggie Murley, the consultant surgeon taking the round, noticed my embarrassment He jumped to my aid with words I clearly remember to this day and in his penetrating falsetto voice exclaimed; 'I've seen this lady on the ward and she wouldn't give anyone a thrill'! This was greeted with howls of laughter that let me off having to explain my delicate position. Many years later I reminded him of this episode when we were part of the same team of travelling examiners in Sri Lanka. He also remembered it and claimed that he had sensed the cause of my embarrassment over the question.

It was during my time as house surgeon to the Royal Northern Hospital that I became engaged.to be married. I now had to seriously consider my future. Up to now I had existed on the meagre income of a house man. It was more like pocket money than a salary. Whatever specialty I decided to take up was going to mean at least six years of further training and poor pay but at the end of the period one could reasonably expect to become a consultant, provided one passed the necessary examinations. In those days the pay of those in hospital training posts was little more than that of a nurse. Unless one had a wife who earned a reasonable income, or wealthy parents, by the time one became a consultant one was inevitably in debt. It was for this reason that so many consultants found it necessary to engage in private practice once they were able to do so. When I qualified I was determined to be different. In my enthusiasm for the principles of the NHS I had decided that if I became a consultant I would eschew private practice and devote myself, fulltime, to curing the sick. Now I had become engaged and I was forced to consider the financial implications of getting married, it became obvious that unless I won the football pools I would be heavily in debt by the time I had completed a lengthy training programme.

At this point fate tapped me on the shoulder. After one particularly trying morning in the out patient clinic and faced with a number of unexpected bills following a lively party in the mess. I picked up a copy of the journal of the Association of Anaesthetists that was lying on the table. On the front cover was the message that was to determine my future. Under the flamboyant Association's coat of arms was the inscription, 'In somno securitas'. Had I only paid more attention during my Latin lessons I would have not made the mistake I did. Or perhaps it was because I was looking for a sign from God to help in determining my future and render me solvent, that I translated the Latin to mean 'There's money in Anaesthesia'. The die was cast; I would give up my ambition for a career in surgery. No more cutting and sewing for me, as my anaesthetist friend at the Gordon Hospital had pointed out, I had the right academic background and scientific training to make a good anaesthetist and as I was getting married, I would need the money.

Anaesthetists have always had an ambivalent attitude towards surgeons. It comes from their mutual dependence whilst, at the same time, acknowledging that the primary responsibility for the patient's treatment lies with the surgeon. It is like a marriage in which each partner tries to establish that it is his or her contribution that is most important to the happy outcome of the liaison whilst accepting that only one of them is the actual 'bread winner'.

It was in this vain that I gave an after dinner address to a meeting of cancer surgeons and their guests. Having told them how I had been seduced into anaesthesia by misunderstanding the Association of Anaesthetist's motto, I suggested that suitable logo for the surgeons would be 'Ubi semen ibi mensus'- as you sow(sew) so shall you reap. Unfortunately only one person out of the hundred or so diners understood the pun; he was the Bishop of London and, unlike most surgeons, he had studied Latin.

On the day I came to the end of my six months at the Royal Northern, McNeil Love presented me with a copy of the latest edition of his book. He inscribed the fly sheet with words of generous praise of my qualities as a house surgeon, then turning to me before he completed the dedication, he asked 'what did you say your name was?' I realised that in spite of my best efforts my surgical skills had failed to make a deep and lasting impression upon the great man. Perhaps I would have more success as an anaesthetist. Reginald Murley provided me with an excellent reference to help me to get my first trainee post in anaesthesia although he could not resist remarking that as a surgeon I showed all the attributes necessary for an anaesthetist!

Chapter Five

Anaesthesia

There is little doubt that, in 1956, anaesthetists were amongst the second class citizens of the medical fraternity. Indeed, legally you did not have to be a doctor to administer an anaesthetic. It was noticeable that when King George Sixth was operated upon by the Westminster surgeon, Clement Price-Thomas, the bulletins on the King's condition were issued over the names of his physician and surgeon, the name of the anaesthetist did not appear. Neither the operation nor the post operative recovery would have been possible had it not been for contributions of anaesthetists, past and present. In the medical establishment of the day the anaesthetist was seldom mentioned. Neither the anaesthetist nor his assistant received personal commendation from the Royal Establishment although somewhat belatedly the senior anaesthetist was awarded a CVO. It was the anaesthetist who stayed up all night ministering to the sick patient after an operation but inevitably, it would be the surgeon who was awarded the credit.

My decision to take up anaesthesia was reinforced by the realisation that there were developments taking place in the field of clinical measurment and in pharmacology that were transforming the speciality into a science. It was no longer a matter of putting patients to sleep so that the surgeon could remove bits of them, it was becoming an applied science. The day of the GP anaesthetist was over. It was no longer necessary to shake one's head sadly when things did not go according to plan and blame the patient's frailty, we now had the tools that allowed us to find out just what had gone wrong and why. If I were to have the opportunity to exploit this development I felt I had to join the most scientifically orientated department of anaesthesia in the country. The choice lay between Oxford and the Westminster Hospital departments. Both of these were at the forefront of anaesthetic research and teaching. My first choice was Westminster where I was known and where I had trained. However, at the time the competition for the Senior House Officer training post was intense, there were some fifteen candidates for every trainee post, but I had the inside track and, after an agonising interview, I was awarded the position of Senior House Officer.

The distinguished consultant staff included Geoffrey Organe (later Sir Geoffrey), J.B. Wyman and Cyril Scurr. Organe held every important post in National and International anaesthesia. He was a master politician, adviser to the Ministry of Health and a very charming, if rather shy, man. J.B. Wyman introduced several new techniques into anaesthesia but is best remembered as the Dean of the Westminster Medical School. Cyril Scurr became Dean of the Faculty of Anaesthesia and President of the Association of Anaesthetists. Like me he enjoyed research and he became my scientific role model. He had an acerbic wit which he used to great effect against difficult surgeons and incompetent housemen.

At that time the junior staff consisted of one senior registrar, two junior registrars and three senior housemen. Together with a four consultants we covered the four operating theatres at Westminster Hospital, a dedicated eye theatre, the X-ray department, the Westminster Children's Hospital and occasionally, the Gordon and All Saints hospitals Today, thanks to EU regulations and various government efficiency drives, there are more than twenty two consultants and about fifteen junior staff to cover much the same sort of work load. We all worked very hard for up to fifty hours a week. Nevertheless, in the six years I was a trainee at Westminster we produced about 100 peer reviewed research papers, five of which won National Research Prizes, two were mentioned in the twelve most important papers published by the Association of Anaesthetists in the past 25 years. We introduced many new anaesthetic techniques, we produced eight text books of anaesthesia and members of the staff, in addition to holding all the important posts in the governance of anaesthesia, examined for the postgraduate fellowship. It was a powerhouse of anaesthetic endeavour. It was an Internationally famous department that always hummed with activity and novelty.

In those days it was not unusual in the department to use one of the housemen or registrars as a volunteer guinea pig for experiments. I can remember one occasion when Bill Paton (later Professor Sir W Paton, Regius Professor of Pharmacology at Oxford) and Geoff Organe wanted to try out the muscle paralysing properties of a new chemical, C5, that Paton had produced, the volunteer selected was the senior registrar. The drug seemed to be totally inactive. It had little effect on the registrar's muscle strength so he was un-strapped from the monitoring apparatus and relieved of his guinea pig task. As soon as he started to stand, however, he collapsed in a crumpled heap. His blood pressure plummeted and he fainted. Paton had produced the first potent antihypertensive drug. It was the fore runner of the drugs used today to treat high blood pressure which save millions of lives each year.

When Cyril Scurr rediscovered an instrument, made by the Germans during the war to measure the concentration of CO_2 in the atmosphere of U-boats, he tried out its accuracy on various members of the staff, before using it to demonstrate the relationship between the depth of breathing and the CO_2 content of the lungs. Ingenuity and originality were the hallmarks of the department.

In Training

I was particularly lucky in training as an anaesthetist at one of the most exciting times in medicine. Anaesthetists were no longer 'licensed poisoners' as they were often dubbed, they were practising scientists. As new drugs and techniques were introduced, each anaesthetic became something of an experiment which could be monitored and controlled, thanks to the many new monitoring tools that were introduced.

Unfortunately the public appreciation of the important role of the anaesthetist took some years to develop. For many years, most thought of the anaesthetist as a cross between a technician and a surgical assistant. So ingrained was this perception, even with the older members of the anaesthetic staff, that I can remember one of the elderly consultants explaining to me, when I was a registrar, that it was important never to 'upstage' the surgeon and always to make sure you drove a less expensive car than the surgeon. On another occasion, when I was administering a local anaesthetic block for a surgical procedure, the patient ask me if I was a proper doctor, when I told her I was she asked if I did general practice?(many anaesthetists at the time were part time GPs). I told her I didn't. She then asked what else I did;-did I do children's clinics? When I explained I spent all my time putting patients to sleep and caring for them during surgery she snorted - 'and you had to train to be a doctor for that'?

The six years I spent in training saw the introduction of new treatments that had only been dreamed of in previous times. Open heart surgery, replacement of diseased blood vessels, artificial joints, heart, lung. liver and kidney transplants and a range of new diagnostic and therapeutic procedures, carried out in the X-ray department, often in the dark. It was the time of the Intensive Care Unit and of pain free, post-operative convalescence. Without simultaneous advances in anaesthesia many of these treatments would not have been possible. Each one of them demanded a new anaesthetic approach and new skills from the anaesthetist. I can remember the long debate, in the Medical Committee that ran the hospital, when we suggested that a Recovery Room should be set aside next to the operating theatres. Older surgeons suggested that it should be considered an anaesthetic failure if the patient was not awake enough to press the lift button himself after an operation and that a recovery room would be waste of space. Whilst a very flattering verdict on the excellence of the anaesthetics at the hospital, it reflected the current opinion of the day that the operating theatre was a place where surgeons cured patients. They resented the idea that the anaesthetist also played an important part in the process.

As one of the junior trainee anaesthetists in a teaching hospital in the forefront of all the advances in surgery, it was usually left to us to meet the problems presented by the new surgical techniques that were being developed. One was expected to cope with any new demand. The consultants were available for advice but they seldom became involved in any new experimental techniques. The emergency work, often the most demanding of all anaesthetic practice, was essentially covered by the registrars. It was very unusual for a consultant to be called in at night unless it was for a private patient or for political reasons. As a result we learnt to make our own decisions, based on a knowledge of physiology and therapeutics, rather than following a protocol or instruction manual. We learnt quickly and we learnt well. It turned every trainee anaesthetist into a practising scientist. This fact was recognised when the new post graduate qualification for anaesthetists was established and physiology and pharmacology were made the principal subjects in the first part of the examination.

One of the big changes in anaesthesia was caused by the introduction of the muscle relaxant drugs. The introduction of curare into anaesthetic practice in 1946-7 marked a turning point in British anaesthesia. Because it paralysed the patient it necessitated the anaesthetist taking control of the patients breathing. It soon produced a significant reduction in anaesthetic mortality. Its use resulted in a much more rapid and pleasant recovery from anaesthesia. Even more importantly, it kick started the scientific study of respiratory physiology for, once one took control of a patient's breathing, one assumed a role normally taken by the patient's brain. It was essential to know how much ventilation each patient required. This became particularly important during the winter fogs that were especially bad in the winter of 1956-7. They brought dozens of patients suffering from breathing difficulties into our hospital. Together with the pulmonary physicians, the anaesthetic registrars set up a special Respiratory Unit ward to cope with the problem. It was largely due to the various techniques and gadgets that we developed that the unit became permanent and some years later, blossomed into the Intensive Care Unit. In 1964, we organised a demonstration of our techniques at a special meeting of the Faculty of Anaesthetists on Respiratory Care, at the Royal College of Surgeons. It was whilst driving back to the hospital after the meeting that I remarked to a fellow trainee, Roger Manley, that provided a source of compressed gas was available, it should be possible to use a pressure valve to turn the constant jet stream issuing from the pipe line, into an intermittent flow suitable for resuscitating patients. By the following Monday, Roger had produced the first prototype of what was to become the most popular ventilator in the UK, the Manley Ventilator.

Many operations require careful and accurate dissection. None more so than cancers involving vital structures such as nerves and arteries. The problem for the surgeon was that too often blood, constantly oozing from minute blood vessels, obscured his view. It was J.B. Wyman who saw the possibility of using a new drug C5, to deliberately lower the patient's blood pressure, as a way of minimising this problem. Wyman tried it out on a patient undergoing a delicate neck operation (no ethics committee approval was necessary, neither was informed consent). It worked brilliantly; when the patient was tilted head up blood pooled in his lower limbs and the blood pressure fell dramatically. When the operating table was flattened the pressure came back to normal. It was the start of hypotensive anaesthesia. It also provided the members of the junior staff with an opportunity to study the relationship of the blood flow to vital organs and the blood pressure. It made us realise that the blood flowing to an organ per minute was more important in keeping the body functioning than actual blood pressure.

The technique of hypothermia, (cooling the patient by packing him in ice) came into vogue initially to make intra cranial operations safer. We extended its use to heart and kidney operations. The technique gave us a chance to find out how cooling the patient affected the activity of the brain and heart. I spent many hours packing bags of ice around the patient's body in an ice cold operating theatre during these studies. I soon learnt to wear long johns under my operating garb.

I can well remember the first time we attempted to replace a leaking aneurysm in a patient's aorta. At the time it was an operation only attempted in a few centres in the World. Before the operation became widely established a leaking aortic aneurysm meant certain death.

Today the surgeons replace the diseased vessel with a preformed, leak proof prosthesis. We had to make do with a hastily prepared graft made by a theatre sister out of a terylene shirt. The criss- cross pattern of the shirt was clearly visible on the graft we used. Although it was soaked in a bowl of blood in an attempt to pre clot the graft, it leaked badly for about an hour necessitating a massive infusion of blood. The operation took five hours to perform. The post operative course was complicated but the patient survived. He was well enough six weeks later to take the surgical staff out for dinner (the anaesthetist, who had stayed up all night adjusting the blood and fluid balance, was not invited).

In spite of the many varied research projects undertaken during my training, it was the poison from the jungles of South America, curare, that became my major interest. This came about as a result of two experiences I had whilst a senior registrar on rotation to Kingston Hospital. Both of these caused me considerable anxiety and discomfort. The first was a very sick patient who failed to breathe properly after the operation in whom I had used a very small dose of a curare like drug to paralyse the patient. At the end of the procedure I gave a dose of the reversal agents which should have antagonised the effect of the of muscle relaxant but they failed to work properly. It was some years before I established that the cause of this increasingly common complication of these drugs was not due to the drugs themselves but to the necessity to ventilate he patient artificially when they became paralysed. The other experience occurred when I included a tiny dose of curare with the local anaesthetic I had used in order to anaesthetise a patient's arm so that the surgeon could reduce a fracture of the wrist. These fractures can be difficult to reduce in strapping young men due to muscle spasm but thanks to the small dose of curare the spasm was easily overcome. At the end of the operation the local anaesthetic wore off quickly but, to my consternation, the paralysis continued for almost an hour. When I tried the effect of a similar injection of curare on myself I found the muscle paralysis lasted for about an hour and it was three hours before I could do up the buttons on my shirt!

I remained a trainee and member of the non consultant staff at Westminster for six years. During that time I spent a year in the USA at the Washington University in Seattle, as a Fulbright scholar, studying research techniques and pain treatment. It was a formative time during which I metamorphosed from an unsure probationer into a competent anaesthetist with proven skills in research and teaching. As a result of the research I carried out at the University of Washington I found myself invited to talk at conferences and meetings in various parts of the world. Eventually I was appointed a consultant to the department of anaesthetics at Westminster Hospital before leaving for another stint in America, this time as a visiting professor, at Stanford University in California.

Surgery

Westminster Hospital surgeons had pushed the boundaries of operability in patients with cancer of the lung to their limits, So it was natural that they should be in the forefront of cardiac surgery when operations on the heart became possible. As a result many overseas visitors flocked to Westminster Hospital to see this evolving new speciality being carried out. Charles Drew, the cardiac surgeon, had developed a technique which allowed him to perform open heart surgery using profound hypothermia. This involved cooling the patient down by perfusing him with cold blood to a point where the brain ceases to function and the EEG fails to register any activity. At this point the heart stops beating and the blood pressure falls. It was during the period of suspended animation that ensued that the surgery was carried out on the still, ice cold heart.

In all the initial experiments in dogs we never managed to produce an animal that survived more than an hour or two using this technique. Today this would have prevented Charles from attempting the operation on patients and it would have put back the use of hypothermia in cardiac surgery. It was only a brave and supremely confident surgeon who would have proceeded to operate on a patient without having a single survivor from his work in animals. However, Charles had established that his technique worked in sick patients and had carried out many successful operations by the time we were visited by a team of Russian cardiac surgeons together with their interpreter.

It was not a simple technique and it required considerable patience. On this particular occasion all was not going well. The electrical monitoring equipment was mal- functioning and it was impossible to know whether the patient was cold enough to start the surgery. The constant bombardment of rather bizarre questions from the Russians, through their interpreter, finally made

Drew snap. He turned on the technicians running the bypass accusing them of being incompetent. He then made scathing remarks about the ability of his assistants. I thought it was a grossly unfair for him to humiliate the technicians, in front of distinguished visitors, especially as they were not in a position to stand up for themselves. I slipped out of the theatre and made for the changing room where, as I had expected, the Fedora hats so loved by the Russians were laid out. I secreted a note in the hat band of the nearest Fedora with the message saying 'I wish to seek asylum in the Soviet Union' and signed it, Charles Drew. My joke was discovered some days later when a member of MI5 came to question the surgeon. I don't think he ever forgave me for that incident although he did graciously apologise to the assistants he had abused.

Drew's technique was a fascinating physiological experiment. I was anaesthetising for him on one occasion when a distinguished American anaesthetist came to watch the proceedure. Professor Francis Foldes was a leading light in International anaesthesia and he was fascinated by what he saw. When the patient's brain temperature reached 15 degree Celsius, the EEG went flat, the heart stopped beating and all signs of life were extinguished, he turned to me and bet me ten dollars that the condition would prove irreversible. Fortunately he was wrong and I received an easy ten dollars reward.

Charles Drew was invited to give a demonstration of his technique of profound hypothermia at an International Surgical meeting in Dublin and he asked me to be his anaesthetist. We duly arrived with our van load of equipment which was to be set up at the St Vincent's Hospital which, in those days, was on St Stephen's Green. I visited the patient before hand and studied his notes. He was very sick and had been in and out of cardiac failure over the past year. He had now deteriorated to the point where his life was seriously threatened. It was then that I learned that whilst we were performing the operation it would be televised and displayed to the thousand or so surgeons in a nearby hall at the College of Physicians. I learned that a doyen of American cardiac surgery, Denton Cooley, would be giving the commentary and passing on any questions, from the audience, to Charles Drew during the operation. Knowing the short fuse of a stressed Charles Drew I sensed trouble ahead but there was nothing I could do. The Irish technicians set about assembling the apparatus which, in all fairness to them, they had not seen before. The first problem was the electrical connections; none seemed to fit;-all the plugs had to be changed. Their way of testing the equipment was to plug the apparatus into the mains, switch it on and see if it went bang. On more than one occasion it blew all the fuses in the hospital. The other problem was the water blanket on which the patient was placed whilst on the operating table. We used the circulation of ice cold water through the blanket under the patient to help speed up the cooling process. It was not until the operation was underway that we discovered that they had attached both the inlet and outlet tubes of the blanket to the pressurised source of water.

On the day of the demonstration, I anaesthetised the patient, set up the intravenous and arterial lines and attached the various monitors that indicated the patient's temperature, EEG and ECG. The patient was positioned on the water blanket on the operating table and Charles and his assistant appeared gowned and gloved. The closed circuit TV transmission was started. At first all went well, the heart was exposed the canulae inserted and Charles instructed that cooling should start. The water started to flow into the blanket and the pumps, draining the heart, started to churn. It soon became obvious that something was wrong with the water blanket. It started to swell, the patient started to get higher and higher on the operating table as water entered the blanket from both the input and the output hose, causing it to fill like a balloon. As the patient's chest rose to approach the level of his chin, Charles had increasing difficulty in operating. Denton Cooley repeatedly needled a stony faced Charles Drew by asking him why he was operating with the table so high. Then there was a loud bang and the blanket burst sending water cascading over the floor. The patient seemed to visibly deflate; he sunk down on the ruptured blanket It was then that I became aware of the next problem. The water had short circuited the monitoring equipment and I had no means of knowing what the patient's temperature was. I could hear Cooley asking Charles what the temperature was in the patient's nasopharynx; Drew turned to me and all I could do was to put my hand on the patient's forehead and guess. I kept saying the temperature was not low enough to stop cooling; to have operated at too high a temperature would have courted disaster. I played it safe and my guesses paid off. All was well, the patient survived. Charles only discovered what had happened after the patient was safely back in his bed. He had been sorely tried by some of Cooley's caustic comments about his technique. In one riposte Drew turned on Cooley and described Cooley's heart lung machine, his pride and joy, as like a load of gramophone records revolving in a milk drum!

That night I slept on a make shift bed in the sister's office, in St Vincent's Hospital, with an Adam fireplace as my headboard, so that I could look after the patient whilst the surgeons went off to celebrate their success. Such is the life of an anaesthetist.

The next night in Ireland was a gala dinner. It was then that I discovered that the dress for the dinner was to be formal. As no one had told me about the dinner I did not have my dinner jacket with me. When my Irish host heard of my problem he said that I should not worry, I could borrow his brothers outfit. I was assured he was much the same size as me. The suit was delivered fifteen minutes before we were due to be picked up from the hotel. When I put it on I found the waist was at least four inches too big and the trousers ended two inches above my ankle. When I saw his brother the next day to return his clothes I found he was much shorter and fatter than me. Nevertheless I enjoyed the dinner, meeting many old friends from my time in the States. The only real difficulty was when they played the Irish National anthem and I was obliged to stand up. It was only by wedging my trousers against the edge of the table that I prevented an embarrassing exposure.

One of the more unfortunate experiences when working with the cardiac unit fell on one of my junior colleagues who was deputed to run the pumps that kept the blood circulating as the patient cooled. Unfortunately on that particular morning he was suffering from the acute after effects of the chicken vindaloo curry he had eaten the night before. Charles Drew failed to notice his repeated absences from the theatre. It was when his demands 'to go on bypass' were ignored he discovered my colleague was not at the pumps. The unfortunate victim had been obliged to seek urgent relief in the nearest toilet. As a result of that episode a rule was made that no junior doctor was allowed to eat curry before he was due to play any role, however minor, assisting in a cardiac operation.

I always maintained that Charles Drew owed me a debt of gratitude. Without my modification of his original cooling system, his lengthy operations would have been impossible. The difficulty arose because, in the early apparatus, the patient's blood was pumped through long metal tubes as they lay in a four foot length of plastic guttering. Ice was packed around the tubes so that the blood was cooled during its passage through the tubes. As the ice melted the water drained from the hole in the guttering that would, in domestic circumstance, be connected to a drain pipe. The problem was that as the water constantly dripped from the gutter over the course of an hour or so the drip, drip noise had a disastrous effect on the surgeon who was approaching the prostatic age. He found that he could seldom last the four or more hours of an operation unless he severely limited his fluid intake. By attaching a comfort tube, from the gutter to below the level of water in the collecting bucket, I solved the problem of Charles Drew's bladder. I maintain that it was thanks to this modest invention that cardiac surgery was able to flourish at Westminster Hospital.

Shortly after the introduction of the Drew technique, it was decided to film the operation. A quiet Sunday was chosen and we all readily gave up our time to help promote Drew's fascinating new technique. There was re-take after re-take before we eventually successfully concluded the operation, some six hours later, in time for tea. It was some days later that we were informed, by a rather sheepish film company executive, that the lens cover had been left on one of the cameras throughout the day. Eventually, the film was made and resulted in the cardiac unit receiving a very generous donation for research.

Some years later, when I was a visiting Professor at Stanford, I found myself working with another pioneer of cardiac surgery, Norman Shumway. It was Norman who deserves the credit for introducing cardiac transplantation although the real breakthrough was, as in all transplant surgery, the development of safe immuno-suppressive drugs that prevent organ rejection. Shumway's unit did all the basic research and they produced several dogs that survived their heart transplantation. Unfortunately, the ethics committee at Stanford had warned them of the risk of being charged with manslaughter if they removed the beating heart, even from a brain dead patient. It was only after Barnard successfully carried out the operation in South Africa, using Shumway's technique, that Shumway was given the green light to carry out his operation at Stanford.

Although few would go back to the days before there were ethics committees scrutinising research proposals there is no doubt that their inherently cautious approach delays and in some cases prevents, new life saving techniques being introduced.

The following year Barnard visited Stanford whilst I was anaesthetising a cardiac patient for Shumway. Norman was obviously annoyed that Barnard had courted and received world wide acclaim for carrying out the first heart transplant using the technique which he had spent several years of his life perfecting. Shumway looked up from the patient on the operating table, grudingly acknowledged Barnard's presence and carried on operating. He deputed the most junior member of his team to show the visitor around and take him for lunch. One can understand Shumway's frustration; it was not as though he had lost the race to be the first to perform a heart transplant, it was that Barnard had used his technique, one he had been prevented from using, to win the race. This display of pique was quite unlike Shumway who was probably the most easy going cardiac surgeon I ever met. He made cardiac surgery look simple and hated anything that complicated surgery unnecessarily. Many of his patients were out of bed and walking the day after major cardiac surgery. He was fortunate to have a great team of assistants including Fogarty, the man who started coronary endarterectomy. Fogarty was already established as an inventor before he took up medicine. He had patented a revolutionary new gearbox which had made him independently wealthy.

It is seldom realised that impetus and funding for the initial heart transplant programme was due to the Physicians at Stanford. Some years earlier, they had shown that Hodgkin's lymphoma, a diagnosis that sounded a death knell to my generation of students, was a disease of the lymphatic system that started in the thymus, a large gland that sits behind the top of the sternum. They demonstrated that the disease spread out from the chest to affect other glands. They found that strong radiotherapy to the chest could halt and in many cases cure, the disease. The problem was that the fierce radiotherapy, in this position, often affected the heart causing its muscle to become progressively more and more fibrotic severely restricting the amount of blood it could pump out. It was the need to find some way of saving the lives of these young patients, cured of their lymphoma but dying of cardiac fibrosis, that kick started the cardiac transplant programme.

As an anaesthetist I have watched the progress of cardiac surgery over its first fifty years. It started with surgeons, such as Sir Rusell Brock in London blindly inserting a cut down scalpel blade, attached to his index finger, into the cavity of the beating heart to relieve the narrowing of a scared mitral valve. It progressed to the point where cardiac transplant surgery has now become such a straightforward operation that, in some centres, it is performed by registrars. Initially, open heart surgery carried a mortality rate of up to 25% but today, a fatality during surgery is a rare event. In between there was such innovative techniques as surface cooling and profound hypothermia. In the early days it was carried out almost exclusively for the relief of defective heart valves or congenital abnormalities. Coronary artery surgery came many years later, after the heart bypass techniques had been greatly simplified and the mortality of cardiac surgery reduced. Surgical intervention in the treatment of coronary artery disease was always second best to prevention or drug treatment. Due to our better understanding of the causes of coronary artery disease and more imaginative interventions, it is becoming less and less necessary. Behind the scenes, in the diagnostic departments, cardiac catheterisation and angiography have developed from what was initially a hazardous challenge to a routine procedure. This has changed the nature of the cardiac surgeon from the Prima Donna featured in television series, such as Your Life in their Hands, who was expected to display temper tantrums, into the more placid surgeon who today carries out, what has become a routine surgical procedure. Cardiac surgery has been demystified.

General Surgery

Our Professor of surgery was my friend Harold Ellis. He is one of the best medical communicators I have known. He attributed his manual dexterity as a surgeon to having been born into a family of dressmakers. He attracted a vast array of overseas visitors who came to watch him at work.

On one occasion he was entertaining a group of five Russian surgeons and their interpreter during an operation to replace a leaking abdominal aorta with a graft. It is not an easy procedure as the stitches frequently cut out of the cheesy walls of the diseased blood vessel making it difficult to get an accurate water tight join between the graft and the blood vessel. Harold was having a sticky time. To add to his difficulties the surgeons were bombarding him with questions, relayed through their interpreter. One could see his patience was wearing thin. When once again the sutures cut out and blood welled up in the wound, Harold had had enough. He put a large swab in the wound and turned to the interpreter saying;- 'Today is Tuesday' this was duly repeated to the surgeons in Russian and the surgeons wrote it down in their little note books. He said 'You will notice I am operating with my left hand'; he was left handed. His words were duly translated and written down by the Russians. He went on to explain that his assistant, who was also left handed, was also using his left hand. Finally, he said 'my nurse is using her left hand'. She was pressing on the swab in the wound with her left hand. 'Gentlemen' he exclaimed 'we train all our surgeons to be ambidextrous; on Monday they use their right hand, today being Tuesday, they use their left hand, tomorrow they will again use their right hands and so on'. These words of the master were duly translated and copied down by the Russians and their message may be being applied to surgical trainees in Moscow to this time, for all I know.

Professor Harold Ellis delighted in being a no nonsense general surgeon. He was one of a dwindling band of surgeons who would take on any surgical procedure that presented itself. His aphorisms, constantly repeated to generations of medical students, became a by-word and they would reappear, in various unsuitable circumstances, in the medical school pantomimes. Harold positively enjoyed surgery. His operating sessions, which were usually laced with amusing historical anecdotes, were always masterly demonstrations of his surgical skills. He was one of the most popular teachers of surgery.

Surgeons have been accused in the media of short changing the NHS by cutting their operating lists so as to play golf or encourage patients to go 'private' I can not think of single surgeon in all my time in the NHS who did not fight to be allowed to fulfil his operating commitments whenever possible. Indeed they tended to look upon their time in the operating theatre in much the same way as an actor regards his time on a stage. I can remember when, during a strike by ancillary staff, the porters refused to fetch patients from the wards to the operating theatre. The surgeons were frustrated; they felt they were being denied the ability to utilise their talents for the benefit of their patients. Because we were not union members the staff were not permitted to cross the picket line and collect the patients ourselves. Harold Ellis, together with other staff members, joined NUPE so that they could fetch and carry the patients. This action was not aimed at breaking the strike but at making sure that patients had their operations.

Even long after his retirement Harold continued with his love of anatomy by teaching the students at Guy's Medical School for many years after giving up surgery. His books and lectures on the history of surgery have won him world wide acclaim.

Not all surgeons were as able or as positive as Harold Ellis. Some were extremely uncertain and slow, especially when they wandered outside their immediate field of expertise.

Most of our dental surgeons were doubly qualified. Having obtained their dental Fellowship they retrained as doctors and embarked on the long surgical training programme and the surgical Fellowship examination. They were amongst the most qualified surgeons in the hospital. It occasionally fell to them to perform major procedures involving the jaw and the face. As it was outside their routine practice they were often painfully slow. It was said that it was a close run thing between the rate at which they resected a cancer and the rate at which it was growing. In an effort to hint that this was a problem we took to replacing the theatre clock with a calendar. When this failed a chiming clock was introduced and finally, to bring home the point, a camp bed was brought into the operating theatre, In all fairness to them, they were judged against a plastic surgeon whose speed at resecting cancers of the head and neck, was legendary.

Ian Wilson was a master at reconstructive plastic surgery, He started life as a sculptor. He studied medicine in Scotland before he took up plastic surgery. He developed his skills as a consultant in Newcastle. He was attracted to Westminster Hospital because it was a centre for the treatment of soft tissue cancers of the head and neck and he specialised in putting the patient's face back together after the cancer surgeon had removed any offending tumorous tissue.

Up to that time most of the defects caused by the surgery were covered with a thin 'split skin' graft that acted like a layer of cling film, covering the wound but not disguising the defect. Sir Archibald McIndoe used a technique, developed by Gillies to treat airman burned in the war, to move full thickness skin, from the arm or leg, where its loss could be easily covered up, to the area of the defect. This involved raising a tube of skin from the arm or leg and then progressively moving it as a tube from one site to another as it was 'walked' towards the defect. Unfortunately by the time the pedicle reached the site where it was required it was usually about half its original length. It was the genius of Wilson and others to use a technique that based the skin flap, used to cover the gap left when a tumour was excised, on an existing arterial supply. As it was most often used for the repair of facial defects they used the skin of the forehead, based on the temporal artery, just in front of the ear, to repair the defects caused by a facial cancer. As Wilson pointed out, it was not new; a similar technique had been used in India centuries ago

Wilson was a very rapid but bloody surgeon; he well deserved his epithet of 'Tiger Wilson'. It was often difficult to predict the extent of the silent invasive growth of a tumour and to plan how best to reconstruct any defect left when it was resected. Wilson would make up the operation to repair the defect as he went along, especially if he found the cancer was more extensive than envisaged and that the forehead would not provide sufficient skin to cover the wound. Noses would come off, eyes and orbits would be excised in order to make sure all the cancer was removed. As a result it was often difficult to see where the mouth or nose had originally been. If the tube carrying the anaesthetic gases to the patient's lung got in the way of his surgery he would just cut through it causing the anaesthetist to start jumping up and down in alarm. Anaesthetising his patients was a nightmare and a challenge. I tried to avoid adding to the patient's misery by performing a tracheostomy that would prevent them speaking after the operation but on occasions it was the only feasible way of making sure they did not suffocate. So horrendous were many of the resections that the patients were not allowed to have a mirror in their room. Amazingly, although he seemed to push surgery to the very limits, the surgical mortality was very low.

Some of his best results were with badly burned children. As a result of his work some of them were able to return to a normal life in communities that would have otherwise rejected them as freaks.

He was the most challenging of all the surgeons I worked with. As he operated his mask would invariably slip down over his mouth and then down to his chin. Nevertheless, serious infection was very rare. Not infrequently one would notice him shifting uncomfortably, rubbing his abdomen against the operating table. This was usually caused by his failure to tie a proper knot in the cord holding up his theatre trousers. His results were amazing, slowly, over months the patient's face would take shape, a mass of skin would turn into a new nose or ear, or a jaw would be re built.

He had a succession of excellent trainees from around the world. Some became professors in their home country others heads of important departments. One, an Australian, who became a successful plastic surgeon in Melbourne, collected antique furniture during his time in London. His purchases crowded the corridors leading to his room at the Royal College of Surgeons and his pride and joy, a classic old Lagonda car occupied the Vice President's parking space. Eventually he was issued with an ultimatum; to either rent storage or to leave the College. There is no doubt about the affection that all of his acolytes developed for their unpredictable, enthusiastic teacher.

Ian Wilson was a short man, about 5ft 6-5ft 8in tall and one of the several Australian assistants he had was very tall, well over 6 ft 2 in. This made it difficult for them to find a level for the operating table with which they were both comfortable. The Australian would try to be first to the operating table and pump it up. If the table was too low he ended up with a awful back ache after a long operation. As a result when Wilson arrived at the table he would find it almost up to his chin. He would then, ostentatiously, lower the table. A fight would then start, one lowering the table the other pumping it up. On some occasions a more subtle rouse would be employed. Wilson would set the table low so that he was comfortable. Once the operation was under way and he was concentrating on his work, the assistant would gradually pump the table up, doing it so smoothly and slowly that Wilson, whose attention would be totally consumed by the operation, seldom noticed what was happening. On more than one occasion he ended up operating on tip toe.

Today, plastic surgeons have taken the 'vascular pedicle' one stage further, to its logical conclusion. They excise a large slice of skin together with its supplying artery and then join the donor site vessel to one near the area to be grafted. This painstaking technique has allowed pioneering surgery, such as finger and limb transplants to be developed.

During my time as a registrar at Westminster Hospital I regularly anaesthetised for the ENT surgeons. There was one occasion when we were performing an operation on a patient with advanced cancer, to relieve her pain. The operation was interrupted at a crucial stage by a priest arriving in the theatre to administer the last rights to the patient. As the surgeon and I sat on the fringes of this macabre going on he muttered 'this does not look at all good; It's as if God is trying to tell me something'. There was an eerie silence in the theatre during the rest of the procedure. No one dare speak, it was as if a ghost had suddenly materialised and was officiating at some ghoulish ritual. There was an audible sigh of relief when eventually the patient was wheeled out of the theatre alive.

Patients presenting with a fishbone in the throat were a fairly regular ENT emergency. The throat would be X-rayed and if the bone was in a dangerous position it would be necessary to remove it as soon as possible. We had one such emergency on a Friday evening when I was the duty anaesthetist. It was about six o'clock when I telephoned the ENT senior registrar on call asking him to come to the Hospital to remove the fish bone. He lived beyond the borders of London, in Kent. It had taken him nearly two hours, in the Friday evening rush hour traffic, to get home and he envisaged an hour's journey back to the hospital. At the end of a busy week and with his family dinner about to be set down before him, I understood his frustration but the need was real and the operation had to be done. Eventually he arrived back at the hospital, the patient was wheeled into the anaesthetic room and I put her to sleep. As I looked into the patient's throat with my laryngoscope, prior to intubating her trachea with a tube to carry the anaesthetic gases into the patient's lungs, I saw the end of the fishbone protruding from the pit on the right side of the tonsil. It came out easily with my forceps. I was then faced with the dilemma. I had made the registrar forgo his dinner, drive some 20 miles back to the hospital and he faced another 20 miles back home, all for nothing. I felt I could not face him to tell what had happened. So I replaced the fish bone. Unwittingly, when I put it back, I put it on the left side of the larynx. The ENT registrar set about the operation to remove the fish bone. He started searching the fossa on the right of the tonsil for the fishbone. After fifteen minutes he became increasingly puzzled as no bone was to be seen. He began to wonder if it had gone through the laryngeal wall into the tissue of the neck. This disaster would have necessitated a major surgical procedure to retrieve the fish bone from such a life threatening site. I could continue the subterfuge no longer- I shamefacedly admitted what I had done. He was greatly relieved and soon found the bone and removed it. As a gesture of forgiveness we both retired to the Medical School bar.

Not all surgeons live up to the 'action man' stereotype. One of the most dedicated surgeons at Westminster was given to considerable self-doubt. He was ambidextrous and never quite sure whether he should stand on the right or the left side of the operating table, whether he should be radical or conservative, or sew up with this or with that suture. His indecision was often mercilessly exploited by his assistants who would, once he finally made a decision, chip in with, 'on the other hand sir…' This would be followed by another period of soul searching. Fortunately, as soon as he realised his indecision was being exploited he was able to join in the joke and laugh at himself. These incidents were recorded in the anaesthetic record as a DUA; Discussions Under Anaesthesia.

Some surgeons were better at some operations than others. Most had their pet procedures. One surgeon made a specialty of operating upon tumours of the parotid gland. This small gland sits, tucked in behind the angle of the jaw, just in front of the ear, where the nerve that controls the muscles of the face emerges from the skull. He was very good at it and it was a delight to watch him dissect out the filamentous nerves as he separated them from the tumour. It was his insistence that all those around him should join in the general approbation to form a mutual admiration society, that became so irritating. So it was that the next time he canvassed our approval for his skills all of those watching held up two prepared score boards, the one in the right giving marks out of 10 for effort the other for achievement. Even this did not cure him of this habit.

The public image of the surgeon struggling valiantly, against all odds, to save a life is not always reflected in the operating theatre. I can remember a distinguished rectal surgeon performing a sigmoidoscopy upon a 'dowager duchess' whilst she was lightly sedated. She appeared to be tolerating the indignity with remarkable fortitude, when she raised her head from the pillow, looked at the surgeon and in a piercing tone remarked 'young man, does your mother know what you do to earn a living'.

There is no doubt that when all is not going well in the operating theatre the level of stress rises. Requests become commands, polite courtesies are ignored and decisions are made on the spur of the moment that are occasionally ill considered. One such occasion occurred when I was anaesthetising a sick patient undergoing a major surgical procedure. As the surgeon was removing a huge cancer, blood started pouring into the wound from somewhere under the tumour and out of reach of the surgeon. It was up to me to keep up with the transfusion of blood so as to prevent the patient bleeding to death. In those days blood was stored in glass bottles and the only way of increasing the flow was by pressurising the contents of the bottle. To do this we used rubber bellows which were designed to pump air into rectum during a sigmoidoscopy. The pump would be attached to the air inlet of the blood bottle and air pumped into the bottle to pressurise its contents. I asked the anaesthetic sister for a bellows. The first bellows appeared to have been baked in an autoclave and was blocked. I called for a second bellows; that was also blocked. I was now getting desperate and when the third bellows also didn't work, my frustration boiled over, I threw the bellows back at the nursing sister. Fortunately, I managed to set up an additional intravenous line in time to meet the need for a rapid supply of blood. The patient survived. However, the sister reported me for throwing the rubber bellows at her. The Nursing supervisor was duty bound to pass on her complaint to my boss, Sir Geoffrey Organe and he passed it on to the chairman of the complaints committee. So it was that the complainant came before the three members of the committee. The complainant was called in to find herself having to explain why she had failed to make sure vital emergency equipment was in working order. She did not persist with her rather petulant complaint. Sir Geoffrey had appointed me to be the Chairman of the Complaints Board. Today my impetuous behaviour would be likely to result in suspension and a formal independent committee of inquiry. The ability of senior staff to use their discretion as to the merit of a complaint no longer exists. No matter how trivial, all complaints are investigated by a committee whose members often do not appreciate the stress facing those making life or death decisions.

Some of these situations are not without their funny side. At the end of an operation, upon a patient's chest, the surgeon asked that the chest drainage tube be connected to an underwater drain. These drains are commonly used to act as a one way valve after chest operations. They allow any air in the chest to bubble out through the end of the drainage tube as it lies below the level of the water in the bottle. The water acts as a seal and prevents the risk of a sudden inrush of air that might otherwise collapse the lung. Gentle suction can be applied to a second tube to assist the drainage. The underwater drainage bottle was duly produced and I instructed the Australian sister, who was helping, to attach the chest drain to the tube that ended under the water. This left the second tube unattached. Obviously puzzled, the sister said 'what should I do with this tube?' I told her it was for suction. As we did not have the optional low pressure suction device in theatre she became agitated. 'Oh' she said 'should I suck on it until we get a pump?' Never one to fail to exploit a funny situation I encouraged her to do so. There were howls of laughter as she got down on her hands and knees and started sucking on the second tube. She got her own back subsequently by sending me scurrying all over the hospital for a non-existing emergency. I met up with her some years later when she was in charge of the operating theatres in Brisbane. There she took the opportunity of introducing me to the audience at my lecture with her edited version of the story.

We had a succession of very good junior staff from Australia and New Zealand. They generally fell into one of two groups. There were those who took locum posts so as to finance their Grand Tour of Europe, proceeding from one beer festival to another. The other group came to the UK to obtain their UK Fellowship diploma. Many became life long friends, some distinguished themselves academically whilst others became directors of prestigious Australian anaesthetic departments. I was given a memorable party in Sydney when a number of these Westminster old boys and girls turned up to wish me a happy retirement. They were, without exception, conscientious members of the department. Indeed when I was offered the Chair at Westminster I only accepted it on condition I could offer one of these old boys the post as my deputy.

Outside the Operating Theatre

During my first spell in America, as a Fulbright scholar, I spent a year as a research fellow at the University of Washington in Seattle. At the time I had completed only one year as an anaesthetic trainee and had recently been married. It was a fine way to start married life. I remember arriving in Seattle, after a long flight from New York, tired and apprehensive. We did not know what to expect. As a Senior House Officer in England I was on the very bottom rung of the academic ladder. I shall never forget the kindness and thoughtfulness of our hosts. The Professor, Lucien Morris, met us off the plane and drove us to his lovely lakeshore home. They treated us like one of the family, helped us to find a car and a home that we could afford and introduced us to members of the department. The contrast between the warmth of their reception and the aloofness with which the British characteristically greet their guests could not have been greater. Seattle is a beautifully city, it has mountains and lakes and a climate that is not unlike that in England. It was the beginning of an economic boom with Boeing starting to manufacture the new Boeing 707. We were soon at home there. My new wife helped supplement my meagre allowance by working as a shop assistant at a local store. But before she could be paid she was obliged to join the Teamster's Union run by the Union boss, Jimmy Hoffa. He was a sinister figure who later disappeared in suspicious circumstances. The Union meetings were held on 'skid row' down by the docks. Skid row got its name from the practice of sliding the timber, cut from the forests of Washington State, down the steep water's edge into the sea for towing out to the bay where the freighters were moored. In those days, Seattle was a very much a smaller town than it is today. It was named after the Indian chief Seattle who only died during the year we were there.

My wife's sales job was not without complications. Shortly after she started her job she had the accounts department of the store in an uproar. She had used the European way of writing dates; day-month- year, whereas the Americans always put the month before the day. In this way the 10th of August was recorded as the 8th of October. On another occasion she caused considerable amusement by asking a colleague for a rubber. Once her embarrassment subsided it was pointed out to her that a 'rubber' in the States means a condom. They used the term an 'eraser'.

In spite of her income we were hard up and rationed ourselves to two meat meals a week. One evening we were invited to a colleague's house at 8.30pm. We assumed this was for cocktails as Americans tended to eat early. After considerable debate we decided that we would blow our weeks 'going out' allowance on a steak meal so that we could enjoy the inevitable very stiff martinis with my colleague. I can still feel the sinking sensation I felt when we arrived to find that, appreciating that we were hard up, they had laid on a steak dinner for us.

It was a year I will never forget. In spite of being very hard up it was probably one of the happiest years of my life. Everyone we met was hospitable and interested to learn about things English. I was able to carry out my researches in a well equipped laboratory with access to advice from researchers who had experience in many fields. Some of the papers I published with my boss, Lucien Morris, on the research carried out there, are still quoted today.

Nevertheless there were frustrations; we were hard up and every dollar mattered. So it was a cause for some distress when I lost my one and only front collar stud. In England separate collar shirts were *de rigeur* and I had a sensible number of the new drip dry white shirts and separate collars with me but without a collar stud they were useless. I spent several hours going from store to store but no one in America had even heard of a front collar stud. They found the idea of a separate collar 'cute'. Unfortunately no collar studs were found. This meant re-equipping myself with new shirts and one less meat dinner at the local steak house.

Lucien Morris encouraged us to see as much of America as possible during our time in Seattle. In 1958 we travelled down the west coast of America in our old jalopy to visit our friends in Los Angeles. We made a diversion to see the burgeoning new 'hot spot' of Las Vegas. In those days it consisted of little more than The Sands, the New Frontier and Wilbur Smith's Desert Inn together with the Golden Nugget Saloon with its famous cowboy illumination outside.

It was after watching a show at the Desert Inn, whilst walking back to our car, that a man collapsed in front of us. He fell to the ground unconscious and his face started to go puce then white as he struggled for his breathe. I immediately turned him on his side, loosened his collar, cleared his mouth and supported his chin. He took in a few deep gasps but showed no sign of regaining consciousness but his pulse and colour improved. By this time a crowd had gathered around us and one of them bent over and whispered in my ear 'have you got a license to practice in Nevada?'. On his advice I failed to give my name to the hotel doctor when he eventually arrived. These were the days before the 'good Samaritan' laws and had the patient made an imperfect recovery he might have sued me. As a young, enthusiastic doctor it was a sobering experience.

I struggled with the American attitudes to anaesthesia and particularly to the way they used muscle relaxants. In the UK we used large doses of muscle relaxants that paralysed the patient necessitating controlling his breathing. In America, they used small, non paralytic doses, and merely assisted the patient's own breathing. This led to my interest into the effects of too much and too little ventilation. As a result of these experiments I came to recognise the narrow limits within which the various functions of the body can operate successfully. It was the start of my interest in CO_2.

It was during my time in Seattle that I visited Dr John Bonica in nearby Tacoma. Bonica was the guru of pain relief. His book on Pain was the bible for all those engaged in the treatment of intractable chronic pain. We became good friends and he interested me in the various treatments that were available at that time. It was natural that when I returned to London I should practiced some of the techniques he had taught me. I soon became aware that one of the secrets of his success was the aura of certainty he created. My interest in the treatment of chronic pain was fairly short lived. I found that too many of these patients came to depend upon any doctor who took time to listen to their stories of the pain that wracked their body; he became their crutch. I had one memorable patient who suffered crippling back pain whenever he had a tiff with his partner. At first I treated him with epidural blocks, they produced instant dramatic relief. It was when I discovered that I could achieve the same outcome by merely pricking his back with a needle that I realised how much pain is influenced by the patient's belief and the doctor's ability to convince him that he would get better. There is no doubt that the pain blocks we performed did reduce some people's pain but there many in whom it was not the painful lesion but the brain's interpretation of the nervous input from the offending part of their body, that caused their distress. One of the reasons why Bonica was so successful was that all of his patients were assessed by a psychologist as well as a neurologist in a well staffed efficient clinic, before he embarked on any treatment.

I made use of every opportunity to complete my researches during my limited time in Seattle. This would often entail working well into the night. I also worked on some bank holidays, especially Independence Day. After all, I argued, it was merely celebrating one more occasion on which an army of Englishmen had defeated a German mercenary army. What surprised me was that the Professor of surgery was also in his office most of the day. He was a delightful, famous surgeon who made a point of introducing me to any visiting surgical dignitary from Britain as if they were bound to know this very junior doctor because, after all, he came from the same country. On one occasion I watched an unfolding cameo as he tried to pull down the roller blind covering his office window only for it to shoot up as soon as he took his hand away. After several attempts his temper frayed, he opened the window and threw the blind out. Some minutes later he must have thought better of his action, he appeared in the quadrangle, furtively looked around, retrieved the blind, put it under his white coat and retraced his steps.

In those days in America there was no question of obtaining either ethics committee approval for any new technique one tried out-there were no ethics committees. Patient's consent was never considered necessary. If one caused the patient unnecessary suffering or a loss one knew one would be sued. It was operator beware! It was in these circumstances that I persuaded my Chief to allow me try alcohol as an anaesthetic agent. After all it was closely related to ether. He had invented a vaporiser, the 'Copper Kettle' that could vaporise alcohol and we tried it out on two patients. It worked, the patients slept soundly for some time after the anaesthetic and they appeared to recover well, if somewhat 'hung over'. The main trouble was that all the staff in the theatre objected to the all pervasive smell of alcohol. They insisted that if we were to continue with this experiment the alcohol should be given intravenously.

On another occasion I tried an extract of cannabis as an alternative to morphine as a premedication. This seemed reasonable as, unlike the usual opiate based premedication, it was known to reduce the incidence and severity of vomiting as well as allaying anxiety. The experiment was abandoned after the first few patients. One patient insisted on sitting up on the trolley singing at the top of his voice whilst gesticulating wildly to the staff. Another started hallucinating and became quite obstreperous when I insisted on putting him to sleep. Another good idea that didn't work out.

Some years later I hit upon the idea of playing a tape recorded loop to patients who were undergoing operations under light anaesthesia in the expectation that some subliminal message might get through to their brain. The message that was repeated over and over again was 'when you wake up you will not be sick'. Out of ten patients, eight were abnormally nauseous and one was actually sick. It appears that one is unlikely to succeed in implanting a negative message in this way. I dropped this experiment when the surgeon complained he could hear the word 'sick' repeated over and over again and it also made him feel nauseous!

STANLEY FELDMAN

Examining

I never really enjoyed examining; it was too much like a game of Russian roulette for the victim. Passing or failing could depend on one event, too much depended on a single throw of the dice. However, I did my stint as an examiner for the specialist diplomas in anaesthesia, surgery and dental surgery. I gained a reputation, I believe unfairly, for being intolerant of fools and ignoramuses. It was not always easy to distinguish between the student who gave a stupid answer because he was terrified and those who gave a stupid answer because they were stupid. I would try to put candidates at ease by starting with a simple enquiry, such as, what did you eat for breakfast, before testing their knowledge of metabolism. One candidate who presented himself, in a state of obvious terror, seemed vaguely familiar. As it is good practice not to test anyone personally known to you, I asked him 'haven't we met somewhere before?' to which he replied 'yes sir, at this examination last year', there was no reason why I should not go ahead and test him as we had no personal contact other than through the examination. In an effort to put him at ease I said to him 'I see, tell me what was the first question I asked you last year?' 'Oh' he replied shifting uneasily in his chair 'you asked me haven't we met somewhere before!'.

If only the candidates had appreciated how relaxed we were and that we actually wanted them to pass, they would have been less in awe of their examiners. Often we would fill in dull times, when there was a lull in the examination, with a sweepstake on the horses. This would determine who stood the first round of drinks in the pub when the examination finished for the day. As the week of examining progressed we accumulated more and more stories about the silly answers some candidates gave. I can remember one candidate when asked about the essential properties of an anaesthetic vaporiser who insisted that his priority was that it should look beautiful. When asked why he put such a priority on appearance he remarked that he only really liked to anaesthetise pretty people. He was sent for counselling. Some of the best and worst doctors I have examined presented at the Fellowship examinations in Sri Lanka. The teaching at Colombo and Pydradinhea (Candy) was very good, the lecturers at these universities were often trained in the UK or America. Those from the Private Medical Schools in India were often lamentably ignorant. It was some years later that I discovered that entrance to some of these private medical schools depended upon the size of the parent's donation and not upon the candidate's aptitude. A decent sized donation on the birth of a male offspring would not only assure him a place at medical school, it was also likely to determine his final examination grades.

Examining in Dublin was always a delight. Our hosts were always generous with their hospitality. It was impossible not to enjoy their company. The exams were very relaxed. Time hardly seemed to matter. On one occasion the examination was curtailed so that we could finish early as 'the fish were biting' and there was 'just time for a bit of fishing before supper'. Each day, after the examination, the examiners would gather round a large table to discuss borderline cases. In the UK these were serious affairs with papers and viva answers scrutinise to see if an extra mark could be squeezed out to help the candidate. In Dublin these sessions were more personal. 'You can't fail him-he is Jimmy's son' or 'If you fail him he will only take the exam again' and 'he can't really afford to fail he has to keep a wife and children'. As a result the call over would often finish quickly. On one such occasion I found that I had a four hour wait before the plane on which I had been booked, left for London. I telephoned Aer Lingus to enquire if there was an early plane I could catch. 'Ah', I was told 'we've got a 'loovly' plane at that time but its flying from London to Dublin, it's a pity you want to go from Dublin to London'.

In Sri Lanka I examined would be surgeons in physiology. I would ask them if they read the medical journals to which they would invariably say 'yes'. I would then ask if they could tell me what was meant by statistical significance. The would look puzzled, sweat would break out on their brows as they tried in vain to think of what 'significance' might mean. In spite of believing they understood what they read it was obvious that very few read the journals critically. It confirmed the impression that surgeons, in general, are more interested in cutting and sewing techniques, than in science. I could never resist playing with them. I realised that science played a small part in their medical aspirations and it seldom stopped them being good at surgery.

One of the chores that faced the examiners in Sri Lanka was to mark the MCQ papers by hand. This entailed placing a flimsy, transparent plastic master sheet over the candidates completed paper and giving a credit if the box that was ticked on his paper corresponded with that on the master copy. This worked well in most circumstances but when the master copy was exposed to the searing 40 degree C of sunlight, as one sat around the pool marking the papers, it tended to distort and melt. New sets of master copies were urgently required and the examiners were forced to work for hours, in the gloom, after sunset.

It was customary for the six examiners, their wives and the examination secretary to be invited to the British High Commission for a formal dinner during the course of the examinations. When the invitations to the dinner eventually arrived it was noticed that in the bottom left corner it bore the instruction dress- RSR. We were flummoxed, not even our very urbane examination secretary knew what RSR was. He was deputed to telephone the Commission to enquire its meaning. A secretary told him, in an imperious tone, implying that only an ingénue wouldn't know, that it stood for Red Sea Rig. Ah! Now we knew-the only problem was what was Red Sea Rig? Another discrete phone call and we discovered it was dress trousers, white shirt, black bow tie and a cummerbund around one's waist. The hotel tailor was kept busy making cummerbunds.

At the time, I lived very near a fellow examiner and I used to run him home after the examinations had finished. On one occasion we arranged that my wife would meet us for dinner at his house as he was entertaining a visiting Professor from Switzerland. It was not a total success. He was inclined to be overgenerous in his pre dinner cocktails. Whether it was the alcohol or sheer fatigue but the guest professor fell fast asleep at the table after finishing his pint sized dry martini and was totally unrousable. We finished the first course and then the main course to the accompaniment of professorial snores. We put him to bed before the desert. I reminded him of this some years later when I visited him in his new post as Chairman of an American University Department. My story was greeted with quiet amusement. Apparently he had laid out several of his American colleagues with his anaesthetic sized cocktails.

Chapter Six

The Bernard Johnson Adviser

In 1965 I was asked, by the Board of the Faculty of Anaesthetists, if I would undertake the post of, the Bernard Johnson Adviser in Postgraduate Studies.

Bernard Johnson had been a Consultant anaesthetist at the Middlesex Hospital and a member of the Board of the Faculty. He had been a much feared examiner with a reputation that caused candidates to quake with terror and reach for the beta blockers, when confronted with him in the exams. The post of Post Graduate Adviser had been established to honour this man who had terrorised generations of present day anaesthetists. It was intended to be a means whereby anaesthetists, especially those from overseas, could find out what was going on in British anaesthesia. It was a quasi ambassadorial role. It combined the duty of organising the College of Surgeon's Anaesthetic Courses (at that time anaesthesia was run out of the College of Surgeons building in Lincoln's Inn Fields) and arranging post graduate secondments for overseas graduates who wished to further their knowledge by joining a UK department as an observer.

I jumped at the opportunity. I enjoyed teaching and found the company of foreign doctors stimulating and mind broadening. The six years I served as the Adviser were some of the happiest and funniest years of my career.

I not only organised and directed the highly success-ful College courses but I also ran Seminars on topical subjects and organised the courses run by the British Council. I made firm friends with people who later became the leaders of the profession in many countries around the world. This was to stand me in good stead when I was travelling and when on lecture tours and attending International Meetings.

Every Tuesday afternoon I would see aspiring anaes-thetists who sought career advice. It was on one of these afternoons that I interviewed a young Royal Air Force junior medical officer who said he would like to become an anaesthetist. I pointed out how difficult it was to pass the necessary examinations, especially for some one who had last studied anatomy and physiology 5 years ago. I promised if he passed his Primary examination I would help him obtain a training post at my hospital. He passed the examination with flying colours; Peter Barnes went on to become the clinical Director of the Department at Westminster Hospital and a distinguished anaesthetist.

I remember, during the Iraq-Iran war receiving a request for a placement of an Iraqi army anaesthetist in a training programme. I arranged for him to be placed in the University Department in Belfast as he wanted expe-rience in anaesthesia and resuscitation following major trauma, only to be informed by the Iraqi authorities that their army doctors could not be posted to what they described as 'a theatre of war'!

The secondments were not always a great success. Although I always arranged for the post graduates English to be tested by the British Council before they were accepted for post graduate experience in the UK, many got round this by using another doctor who spoke good English to present themselves in their place at the British Council. Another problem was the vast difference in the medical education of the applicants. Post graduates from Romania and Bulgaria often had a poor grasp of general medicine, although they invariably had a British Council letter attesting to their good knowledge of medicine and the ability to speak English. We had a few Burmese doctors referred to us for post graduate training. They seemed to have had virtually no true medical training and arrived with very little financial support. An added confusion was the apparent randomness with which the Burmese appear to chose their names. Thus 'Beautiful Butterfly' might be the son of 'Powerful Elephant'. I became very fond of these soft spoken charming trainees who, when they arrived in the UK, had no knowledge of the Western world, some had never experienced an aeroplane flight or ridden in a train before they were sent to the UK.

I took every opportunity to get to know as many of the post graduates as possible and when appropriate to ask them home to see how a middle class English family lived. I can remember having a group of foreign post graduates to our home one Boxing Day when, after lunch we played monopoly. Our guests from countries behind the iron curtain joined the rest of us in this demonstration of rampant capitalism but our Burmese doctor was so fascinated by the snow that was falling outside that he failed to join in;- he had never seen snow before.

I found the six years I spent as Post Graduate Adviser very rewarding. Life long friendships were established and I came to appreciate the tremendous variation that existed in the standard of medicine that was being practiced in different countries and the very different standards of living enjoyed by the doctors who practiced anaesthesia in these countries. These doctors were the cream of those in their country. Many became the leaders of the profession and some ended up as International stars in the specialty.

There was one occasion when a visiting Chinese professor who had come to spend six months with us to observe our research techniques, volunteered to be the subject of a series of experiments The experiment involved giving repeated, very short electric shocks to the nerve at his wrist and recording the strength of the contraction it caused in the muscles in his hand. He was a stoical character and never winced or moved when the shock was applied, he was my prize volunteer and together we produced some excellent results. Unfortunately on one occasion a switch had been inadvertently activated and unbeknown to us he received a shock that was ten times the normal. He remained unflinching under this torture. It was only the smell of burning flesh that alerted us to what was happening. Professor Xinman Wu was to become the President of the Chinese Society. He remains a good friend.

These were the days before ethics committees and patient consent forms made it impractical to experiment on each other.

One of the doctors I met through my post as Bernard Johnson Adviser, was Jon Spierdijk. Jon came to see me when his appointment as Professor in Anaesthetics at the prestigious Leiden University in Holland had been confirmed. Jon realised that he lacked any background in research and teaching and that to some extent his appointment had been politically motivated. At the time many of the Dutch University anaesthetic departments were serviced either by GPs or by doctors from the Balkans and the reputation of the departments was poor. If Holland was to train and attract good Dutch doctors into anaesthesia they needed a role model who was Dutch. Jon fitted the bill. He came to London to learn how we were training anaesthetists and to see the sort of teaching courses he should be providing. It proved to be the start of a long and memorable association.

Our preconceived stereotypes conjures up a picture of a Dutch man as being a rather portly, fair skinned blond who is dour and humourless. Someone, whose choice of house plants would be Mother-in-laws tongue. Well, Jon was a fair skinned blond but he was tall, had a ready smile and a devastating wit. After a particularly black spell for Dutch anaesthesia, when two patients died from anaesthetic accidents and an anaesthetist committed suicide, Jon was invited to appear on Dutch television to reassure the public. He explained that he thought it was as safe to have an anaesthetic in Holland as to go for a ride in a taxi. When he returned home to Leiden he found his house surrounded by dozens of protesting, angry taxi drivers. The situation looked ugly. Jon invited three of the taxi drivers into his house for a beer. They emerged about an hour later and made an agreed statement to the Press. It read 'after discussions, we have concluded that it would be very dangerous to have an anaesthetic in a Dutch taxi'. The situation had been defused.

STANLEY FELDMAN

Together, we developed a teaching programme for his department including a series of Boerhaave conferences which soon became established as a regular feature of the academic year in the University. It helped attract first class anaesthetic trainees and visiting Professors. It led to the establishment of a research department of international repute in Leiden.

On several occasions we travelled together to present research papers at International conferences. It was whilst travelling to America on one such occasion that Jon boarded the plane some minutes before me. When I eventually arrived on the plane the stewardess met me and took my boarding pass. She showed me to my seat, fixed my seat belt for me and took a blanket down from the luggage locker and placed it on my lap. At this point I smelt a rat; this was more than usual attention for an economy class passenger. It was when I was refused an alcoholic drink with my meal that I discovered why I had received this attention. When Jon had boarded the plane he had asked the stewardess to 'look after my friend he is mentally handicapped'.

On one occasion, during an International conference, when we were being entertained at a smart restaurant in New Orleans by two very senior American anaesthetists, Jon produced a small tape recorder with a message from his youngest daughter for one of our hosts. Soon the conversation got round to the differences between America and Europe and Jon made the sweeping statement that 'American women are naïve'. Our hosts took exception to this all embracing remark admitting some might be but one naïve women does not make all Americans naïve. To prove his point Jon picked up his recorder and marched over to a table in the corner of the restaurant where two young ladies were dinning. He introduced himself, in broken English, as a visitor from a poor University in Holland and explained that he had been asked to interview some Americans about their sex life for the University newspaper, to help offset his expenses. To our amazement they sat him down, poured out some wine and proceeded to relate all their problems to his recorder. It was some 10 minutes before he returned to our table in triumph explaining that the women were nurses from the nearby Charity Hospital and had given him a frank account of their extraordinary sex lives. Our hosts insisted it only proved that some nurses are gullible. This provoked Jon to pick up his recorder once again and sortie over to a couple sitting at another table. Again, he repeated his introduction explaining how European Universities were very poor compared to American ones and they had to find ways to supplement their income. Once again he was given wine whilst the man and his lady friend poured out their sexual history to him. The chat ended with him being invited to see dawn break over New Orleans from the lady's roof garden!

The Boerhaave courses, which Jon and I arranged each year, allowed me a chance to elaborate on the fame of the University in Leiden when I was called upon to open these conferences. I would take the opportunity to recount the history of this famous University which was founded by William the Silent when he raised the siege of the town in the seventeenth century. As a reward for their stoicism he offered them a year without taxes or a University. They chose a University. It soon became a

centre for science. It was here that Professor Sylvius
found what he believed was a cure for malaria which was
affecting the Dutch troops in the East Indies. He made it
from an extract of juniper berries, which were brewed to
give a liquid which we know today as 'gin'. The troops
did not like the taste of this new medicine so they added
cinchona bark extract to take away the bitterness. It was
not the gin that cured the malaria but the cinchona
extract as the physician to the Dutch army, Dr Wienke-
bach pointed out, the cinchona bark they added to the
medicine contained quinine which had powerful medici-
nal effects. On another occasion, I pointed out that the
Netherlands were a maritime nation and Leiden was the
most prestigious school of navigation in the 18 and 19th
centuries. Jonathan Swift wrote, in Gulliver's Travels,
that Gulliver went there to study navigation. I had great
pleasure in pointing out that his Leiden training left
something to be desired as on page two of Gulliver's
Travels he is ship wrecked in Van Deeman's land.

Lecture Tours

One of the first signs that you have 'made it' as a
researcher is when you are asked to talk to this or that
society. It is only when one has scored some success at
these 'away' sessions at places like Birmingham, Dudley,
Crewe and the remoter outposts of anaesthesia in the
UK, that you are tossed a plum- a National or International meeting in a land close by a pleasant holiday
resort. My passport to this world came through the
British Council. Even before I had been appointed a
consultant in the UK I was invited to tour Greece, Israel
and Cyprus for the Council. The Council worked me

hard but it had its compensations. I met the leaders of the professions in these countries and many became life long friends. I came to realise that differences in the calibre and interest of the Council staff determined the sort of reception one might anticipate. In some countries they were more interested in poets than in science and they showed it. My abiding impression of that first trip was of the pride taken by our hosts in their local cuisine. So it was in Greece we had the typical Greek stuffed vine leaves and kebabs, in Cyprus the national dish was meat balls and kebabs and in Israel, just lots of kebabs!

The British Council sponsored my visit to Portugal to speak at the Annual Meeting of the Portuguese and Spanish Society of Anaesthesia. It was at that meeting I met John West who was, like me, working at the Postgraduate Medical School in London at that time. I can clearly remember John's talk about the studies he made on acclimatisation to high altitudes carried out with Sir Edmund Hillary. They planned to winter at the base camp on Mount Everest and to carry out the studies on the Sherpa guides. These investigations involved collecting samples of their expired breath in a bag as they pedalled an exercise bicycle. In order to carry out these experiments it was necessary to block their nose, to make sure they only breathed through their mouths, using special nose clips. Unfortunately he had to abandon the original plan as he found that it impossible to keep the nose clips on the flat noses of the Sherpas. As a result he and his fellow physiologists had to become the subjects of their own studies.

It was during this trip that I became friendly with the distinguished Portuguese anaesthetist, Dr Manuel Silva

Araujo. Some years later we met up again at a conference in London. We were having coffee together when a call came through asking him to phone Lisbon. He explained he was being recalled urgently to attend the Portuguese dictator Salazar. He was particularly surprised at the request as he had been open in his criticism of the dictator and feared that, like others, he might be ordered to a 'voluntary exile' in Angola. He later explained what had happened. It appears that Salazar had suffered a severe stroke and was deeply unconscious and Ciento had been sworn in as his successor. However Salazar lingered on in a twilight world; neither alive nor dead. My friend immediately saw that much of Salazar's problem was that he was not breathing adequately and, being a capable anaesthetist, he put a tube into his trachea and started to assist his shallow breathing. Within an hour Salazar was opening his eyes and although he remained partially paralysed he woke up from his narcotic state. As a result Portugal had two living Presidents. In the three weeks until he finally succumbed to another stroke, Salazar continued to believe he was indeed in charge. The fact that Cientro had been installed to replace him was kept a secret from him.

I was fortunate to be sponsored by the British Council in travels to many countries but the parting of the ways came following a trip to Hong Kong. They insisted, not unreasonably, that I flew British Airways economy class, which meant that in order to fulfil my clinical commitments, I arrived only half an hour before I was due to lecture. To add to the strain there was a formal dinner, in my honour, following the talk. I was young and prepared to accept this had I not observed a fairly junior member of the Council, on the return flight, travelling Business Class at the Council's expense. On another occasion when I was lecturing in Iran the British Council accommodation was in a poor hotel adjacent a run down area of the city into which our Iranian hosts were reluctant to travel. At night one had to step over the body of the house guard who slept outside the bedroom as the previous hotel guests had been robbed at knife point during the night.

It was during this trip that I gave a series of talks at the University in the late afternoon before the end of Ramadan. As there were four talks on successive night to the same audience of over 100 anaesthetists. I tried to end each talk with a 'cliff hanger' question mark so that I would have a ready start to the next day's lecture. I realised that I was replicating Scherazarde's trick she used when telling her stories to the Caliph in the same country.

To celebrate the end of Ramadan (or possibly the last of my talks), there were the usual festivities and we were invited, with the British Council Officials, to dinner at the Professor's house in North Teheran. A Council member picked us up at the hotel and drove to our host's house. The door was open, as is customary, to demonstrate hospitality and we trooped in bearing a small gift my wife had brought with for such an occasion. We were most cordially greeted by our host and given plates of sweetmeat-only, one by one we realised that none of us recognised the host or, come to that, any of the guests seated around the vast room. Slowly it dawned on us we were in the wrong house. Fortunately our British Council minder spoke excellent

Farsi and amid considerable embarrassment, we made a graceless exit, pausing to pick up our gift on the way out.

In one town in Iran we were invited to the magnificent house of the chief of police who delighted in showing us the blocks of opium he had confiscated. His house was decorated by life sized statues of nymphs but every one had been tactfully clothed in running shorts to preserve their modesty.

We have remained good friends of the Professor, who was vice chancellor of the University until the revolution, and have acted in locus parentis for their children when they came to study in England.

Our experiences when invited to travel to Curacao for the Dutch Ministry could not have been more different. They insisted I travelled first class by KLM which meant that my wife, who accompanied me, travelled economy! In those days first class KLM was a treat. The steaks were cooked beside one's seat. I must admit to feelings of guilt about my wife in economy. Our group was accommodated in good hotels. It was during this meeting that I met the only anaesthetist practising in Surinam. He lived on a farm by the Surinam river. This was a shallow river that teemed with piranha fish. He told us how the natives dealt with the difficulty of having their homesteads separated from the best grazing by this piranha infested river. He assured me that they used to send their wives across the river in the early morning and if they were not attacked by the fish they reckoned it was safe to let their cattle cross.

I used to visit America frequently on these trips. I remember visiting the Coca Cola sponsored University of Emory in Atlanta. It had a well deserved reputation for its research output and I enjoyed lecturing there. On one occasion I was taken to visit one of their large hospitals. In one ward I was shown a patient with a large bandage enveloping his foot. They explained that he was in hospital for a gall bladder operation but a patient in a nearby bed had pulled out a gun from under his bed clothes and tried to shoot a visitor as he entered the ward. Unfortunately he had missed the target and shot off two of the toes of the patient with a bandage on his foot.

One of the more extensive tours to which I was invited was organised by the Indian College of Anaesthetists. It started in Bombay then went on to the Annual Congress in Manipal and from there to Dehli and finally to Calcutta. Our hosts had thoughtfully arranged for us to be escorted by a charming Indian doctor. All went well until we reached Mangalore on our way to Manipal. The Indian airline decided it was too fogy to fly which left us with no alternative but to go by road, a journey of some 200 miles. A suitable car was inspected (few of the cars had serviceable tyres) and the driver quizzed by our escort to make sure he licensed to drive. We set off late in the afternoon and travelled at speeds not in excess of 30 mph in order to avoid the pot holes and obstructions on the highway. The real problems started after dark. Although most of the heavy loads were carried in highly decorated trucks there were many camel and ox drawn carts amongst them. After dark the tired animals would just sit down in the middle of the road and go to sleep. As a result our progress became progressively slower and slower as these unlit hazards loomed out of the foggy night. The journey eventually took eight hours.

The fog haunted our trip. We were due to fly from Delhi to Calcutta for the last talk but once again the fog grounded the aeroplanes. We spent 26 hours on Delhi airport before we were finally able to leave. We arrived in Calcutta less than one hour before I was due to give my talk. Our escort had phoned ahead to say we were delayed. He was told that there was an audience of 220 waiting and that the refreshments they had provided for a reception, after the talk, had already been eaten. Our minder suggested that rather than wait for our luggage I should go on ahead to the hotel where the lecture was being held. So, clutching my slides, I took the waiting car to the hotel. I gave my slides to the organiser of the lecture but pleaded for time to have a quick shower and change my shirt (I had not washed for nearly two days and it was steamy hot in Calcutta). He showed me to my room-it had a large internal bathroom of black marble. I quickly undressed, entered the shower and had just soaped myself when all the lights went out. It was pitch black and I was in a hurry. It was dark, the marble in the shower room was black and slippery and I could not find the taps. I found myself sliding about, I banged my head on something, felt scalding water but could not turn the water off. Eventually I found the door. It seemed to be an eternity before I emerged from my own particular Black Hole in Calcutta still soapy but relieved.

It is a lecturer's nightmare that, after preparing a lecture around his slides, he will be unable to show them. I always made sure that my host knew exactly what sort of slides I would be bringing. It was in that high tech. capital of the world, Taiwan, that I came unstuck. I had hardly started my talk when the projector bulb blew and the slide went blank. In spite of all the technical sophistication of the country, no spare bulb was available. I asked for a blackboard or an overhead projector but none was to be had. The slogan 'the show must go on' came to mind, I did my best but it is difficult to describe to an audience what can be shown on a slide.

One of the more interesting lecture tours was that organised by the Chinese Academy of Sciences. I have always found the company of the Chinese doctors fun and looked forward to returning to China for the lecture tour. I was amazed at the transformation since my first visit some 10 years earlier. Often in shabby hospitals, sophisticated surgical techniques were being carried out with considerable success. In Beijing, the doctors were impoverished, the hospitals in poor repair but the operating apparatus was as modern as anywhere in the world. Although acupuncture was still practiced in the countryside and in special hospitals in 1994, the era of native medicine and herbal remedies had past.

The dinners that were arranged were invariably funded by the State and gave an opportunity for the poorly paid doctors to order banquets that, had they been paying themselves, would have been beyond their means. Exquisite fish and lobster dishes, duck's feet, chickens gizzards, camel's foot and pheasant. I drew the line at having the scrawny peacock, chained to the counter of the restaurant, sacrificed for my delectation. The meals were usually accompanied by toasts which were followed by the customary 'yam sing', during which the person giving the toast would down his glass of wine or beer in company with the guest of honour. After six or seven such toasts I had drunk enough. I was feeling pretty drunk. At this point I nominated my minder to take the rest of the toasts on my behalf.

I am often reminded of Beijing when I visit the West end of London in the evening and see the bicycles and rickshaws drawn up at the traffic lights-only today in China one is more likely to see limousines than bicycles and rickshaws. Such is progress!

It is interesting how national characteristics come to influence International meetings. In Italy I was once due to talk first at a meeting scheduled to start at 9.0 am. At dinner, the evening before the meeting, I asked my host what time we should breakfast. 'Oh about 9.0 am' he suggested. I protested that I was due to talk at 9.0am but he assured me it would be alright. He was correct the audience only started arriving at 9.45 and we did not start until after 10.0am.

On another occasion in Spain I was given 45 minutes to talk. I was introduced by the President who not only spoke for 20 minutes but also showed several slides from my paper. Eventually, as I was called to the rostrum and my host turned around to greet me, the microphone that was attached to his lapel became disengaged from its wire and flew off into the audience. There was hectic scramble to retrieve it followed by an emergency repair. That left me only 15 minutes before lunch to give my talk but as the President had already shown many of my slides I had ample time to give a summary before settling down to the real purpose of the meeting, an excellent lunch.

The situation was very different in Switzerland and Germany. There the timing was precise. I learnt not to try to make jokes to a German audience- it is not that they lack a sense of humour but that they do not believe it possible to mix work with pleasure. I only lectured on one occasion in what used to be East Berlin but, unlike in the rest of Germany, I realised a large section of the audience were not following my talk. Only afterwards was it pointed out that most of the older doctors had learnt Russian, not English, as their second language.

One of the most enjoyable meetings was held in Ireland. I can remember one speaker giving a detailed account of the problems she had encountered transporting a desperately sick patient from her local hospital to Dublin, in an ambulance. The patient, she told us, was wheeled into the ambulance on a trolley accompanied by a mobile ventilator to keep him alive. The driver got into the ambulance, revved up the engine and let out the clutch with a bang. The sudden acceleration of the vehicle caused the ventilator which was on wheels and the trolley to shoot backwards bursting open the back door of the ambulance depositing them and the patient, back on the hospital drive. After reconnecting the patient to the life support machine and getting everyone back into the ambulance they set off. She connected the ventilator to the ambulances battery terminals and settled down for the journey. They had barely covered five miles when she noticed smoke coming from the machine. After another mile or so it ceased to work. She had not realised the ambulance ran on 24 volts and the machine on 12 volts.

As a result of my interest in the muscle relaxant drugs, I formed a Study Group, at the instigation of a Sandor Agoston, an engaging and delightful friend who worked as an adviser for the Organon pharmaceutical company. We held the first meeting at Westminster Hospital in 1974, and I was given the job of making suitable arrangements. Unfortunately, although I knew the names of the eminent personalities we were inviting to the meeting, I had not met all of them personally. It was only at the inaugural dinner I discovered that the Dr B.E, Waud, whose work I had admired and whom I had assumed was a man was in fact a very lady like female and an ardent feminist. She exploited my discomfiture, to the full. I don't think she ever believed the error was accidental.

We went on to have meetings in various parts of the world and they became the power house behind the development of new and better drugs. It was the Tokyo meeting that I remember most clearly. My wife and I arrived in Tokyo on the afternoon of the opening dinner. We had not been to Tokyo before and were immediately struck by how different it was from other countries. Every country has its own particular ambience but Tokyo is in a league of its own. The hotel room was lavish but the bed, by Western standards was small, I was a fascinated by the lavatory in the bathroom. It had six buttons and performed a different function when each button was pressed. Button one and it was a bidet, button two made it into a fountain, another button and the seat became hot, then it self cleaned. I did not realise that, after playing with it for some time and moping up the water on the floor, it was getting late for dinner. As a result, although I changed very rapidly I arrived for the dinner after most guests were already seated. The meal was sumptuous, caviar, lobster, birds nest soup, kobhi beef, champagne and French wines. There was an elderly Japanese gentleman sitting next to my wife, who ate and drank nothing, he was so still that had I not observed his chest occasionally rising and falling I would have wondered if he were still alive. I hardly saw his eyelids flicker during the whole time we ate our meal. During dinner our host came up to me and asked if I would give the after dinner speech and introduce some six or seven speakers. I regretted agreeing to his request when he presented me with the list of speakers to introduce-it was in Japanese!. After I protested, he rapidly wrote an approximate phonetic translation for me. I duly gave my speech and then, with considerable difficulty, pronounced the name of the first speaker. Imagine my surprise when the almost dead gentleman, who had been sitting motionless beside my wife, sprang from his chair. He had obvious been preparing himself for this event during the meal by some oriental form of inner contemplation, he walked briskly to the podium, arranged a several sheets of paper on the podium and delivered a ten minute oration, in what I took to be Japanese but which my host assured me was English.

It was an excellent meeting with little free time, although we did manage to slip out of one session, to join some Japanese friends at a nearby restaurant for lunch. The restaurant table had a wooden top on which a large shallow metal dish, containing water, had been placed. Four or five stones, each about the size of a chicken's egg, were arranged in the dish and these supported a large tureen containing a chicken flavoured soup. What fascinated me was that the soup soon started to boil although I could see no means by which it could be heated; the water in the metal dish beneath it and the dish itself was stone cold. I mentioned my puzzlement to our host who said he hadn't ever considered how the soup in the tureen was heated. He also was puzzled so he called over the waitress and asked, in Japanese, if she could explain the phenomena. She hadn't the faintest idea, so the front of house waiter was called, he also had no explanation of the phenomena, so the manager of the restaurant was summoned. We explained the problem. 'How' he was asked 'was the soup heated when there was no apparent source of energy?' 'Simple' was his reply, pointing to a concealed switch beneath the table he continued, 'I switch on this switch and it becomes hot'. We gave up, sat back and enjoyed the meal.

Stanford University California

I had been a consultant for four years when John Bunker, the Chief of the Department of Anesthesiology at Stanford University in California and an eminent researcher, came to spend a sabbatical year at Westminster Medical School. He became interested in the work I was perusing with the muscle relaxant drugs and invited me to become a Visiting Professor in his Department. I jumped at the opportunity as it was where Ellis Cohen was doing some pioneer work on measuring blood levels of the relaxant drugs, such as curare, using radio-active techniques. I duly arrived in Stanford in 1967 for a years secondment. Ellis proved to be generous with his time and friendship and, as a result, my time there proved seminal in developing the techniques I was to use later in my research in the UK.

In 1967, Stanford had one of the first IBM-1800 computers. One needed to use a special computer language, FORTRAN, in order to talk to it. It was housed in a large room, about the size of a squash court, which had to be air conditioned to keep the temperature at a bearable level. It generated enormous amounts of heat from its thousands of thermionic valves. By modern standards it was extremely slow and ponderous and expensive to run. It generated sheets of incomprehensible output. Using a modern, slim line lap top computer today it is difficult to realise how far this evolved from these early computers of forty or so years ago. Nevertheless its ability to perform massive mathematical computations, relatively quickly, proved invaluable.

Stanford was, and still is, an intellectual hotbed. Every Autumn researchers would eagerly search the mail for a letter from the Noble Committee in Sweden telling them of another prize winner to add to the 5 already on the teaching staff. Although it was a highly competitive atmosphere it was also very civilised and friendly. It surprised me how hard people strove in an environment that was, in many ways, an academic and physical Lotus land. I have never attended so many pre breakfast, 7.00 am meetings or seen so many dawns break, as during the year I spent at Stanford. On one occasion a colleague, at a nearby institution in San Francisco, invited me to visit and to see his research. He said he would pick me up at 4.30 which was OK by me as it meant I would have time to look around after lunch. The only problem was that he meant 4.30 am.

All the doctors at Stanford Medical Centre were well versed in the latest medical research so I was not surprised by the enthusiastic way they embraced any potentially life enhancing or fitness regime. Cycling became an obsession and the joggers could be seen on the campus from before dawn until sunset. I was breakfasting with a colleague, who rather daringly ordered fried eggs sunny side up without bacon, of course, as it was considered a toxic food. He then proceeded to carefully dissect out the yolk from the white of the eggs and move them to one side of his plate. He then stopped eating, looked at me and said, rather forlornly, 'I've forgotten which part am I supposed to eat., the white or the yolk?' Certainly there was a robust good health about everyone one met at the University-but then it was a high income, easy living world they lived in.

Whilst at Stanford I was invited to give talks at various institutions in California. I can remember talking in Sacramento, the State Capital, on the British health service and telling the audience about the benefits of the NHS and how well treated were its patients. It provoked an angry disbelief amongst the right wing medical audience many of whom were earning huge salaries, by British standards. It is sad that political intervention has turned the NHS of 1967 into the badly run, bureaucratic, inefficient monolith of today providing imperfect medical treatments for so many patients.

It was at one of these meetings, that of the Californian Society of Anesthiologists, that I made one of those glib remarks which in retrospect cause one to blush with embarrassment. I was a member of a panel of 'experts' answering questions from the audience when I was asked why medical mal-practice insurance was so cheap in the UK whilst it ran into many thousands of dollars in California. My flip reply was that I could only assume that if mal practice insurance was expensive it must be because there was a lot of mal-practice in California. The audience was understandably unimpressed by my answer. Today with a similar 'blame and sue culture' in the UK, insurance levels are now also prohibitively high here, as well as in the States. On another occasion I made a similar off the cuff remark which must have surprised my hosts-it certainly causes me discomfort every time I think about it. After I had given an eponymous lecture at a prestigious University in South East America, the Dean of the Medical School and the Chairman of the department of Anesthesiology invited me out to dine at an expensive restaurant. The Chairman explained that he was retiring at the end of the year and that my name had been put forward as a suitable successor, by the search committee. I was flabbergasted as I had not considered living permanently in the USA. Although the institution was highly regarded, it was in a very hot, humid part of the country and I am always uncomfortable in humid environments. Indeed the outside temperature was 106 degrees F. He explained that in a good year, as head of the department, he could make over a million dollars (this was in 1987). This enormous salary sent my head spinning but I knew the proposition was a non-starter. I loved London, my wife and children were happy there and I was at the beginning of my career. All I could think of in reply was to mumble 'that I didn't think I could take the cut in salary' naturally, he was somewhat surprised. My actual salary at Westminster Hospital at the time was less than £40,000 a year.

In spite of my unintentional rudeness we remained friends and a year later I had occasion to entertain the Chairman to lunch in the Consultants dinning room at Westminster Medical School. As the desert was being served there was a loud bang immediately over the head of my guest; a light bulb had exploded. I have never seen such a display of agility in a 65 year old man as when the Chairman of this famous University department dived under the table. Coming from the South East of America such a bang meant only one thing;-a pistol shot.

Research

My attitude to research has always been that of a practicing clinician. I have never been happy with the idea that all research is about sitting in a laboratory dreaming of finding an answer to a 'meaning of life' type of question, the so-called 'moon-shot' approach. I saw it as the job of clinical research to find answers to clinical problems and to solve these, wherever possible, within the clinical environment. Only when that became impossible was it necessary to resort to laboratory tests. I believed that it was as a result of trying to solve these puzzles that one produced the seed corn of meaningful laboratory based investigation. To some extent this attitude was forced upon me by the lack of basic science facilities within the Westminster Medical School.

At the beginning of my career it was possible to use animals for research but only after having obtained all the necessary permissions. This required lengthy negotiations with Home Office officials and conducting the experiments in approved accommodation. This was expensive, time consuming and difficult to obtain. This problem, together with an abortive initial attempt to use feral cats captured beneath the prefabricated cabin wards at Roehampton Hospital(even thick gloves did not protect one from the teeth and claws of these vicious animals), dissuaded me from experiments involving animals. So it was that very often I ended up experimenting on myself or one of my assistants. I soon discovered that the quickest way to empty a room full of trainee registrars was to ask for volunteers. However, my research assistants often felt obliged to suffer in the cause of the science that we were jointly pursuing.

There was one memorable occasion when I was to be the victim of a test involving the injection of a minute amount of a paralysing muscle relaxant into a needle in my forearm, when the needle became blocked. My assistant picked up a syringe, half full of fluid, and believing it to be saline, proceeded to clear the block by injecting its contents it into the partially blocked needle. Unfortunately, the fluid he injected was a concentrated solution of the paralysing drug we were testing. This became evident when I started to develop double vision, then I found that I could not move my arms or legs or control my tongue. My assistant looked on with amazement as I slumped in the chair and became progressively paralysed. Fortunately I could still, just about, breathe although I could not speak. It was a frightening experience but one which seemed to cause more anxiety to my assistant than to me. He realised that, not having envisaged this sort of complication, we did not have any antidote to hand. It took several very long minutes to obtain the antidote drugs and administer them. Slowly I recovered over the next 20 minutes but it had been a salutary lesson. From that time on we had a full resuscitation set in the laboratory.

We were a close knit family of research workers and enjoyed being part of a successful team. Our Christmas parties were always memorable. Our chief laboratory technician, who was a good artist, would make 'going home presents' for the guests each year. One year it was a game of Snakes and Ladders in which the longest snake would be the most unpopular surgeon and the ladders would consist of events such as 'being referred to intensive care unit' or operated upon by one of the more popular surgeons. Another year there was a colouring book for aspiring surgeons with pictures entitled, A is for adenoids colour me pink, B is for blood colour me red etc. These parties were also the occasion for us to make the annual presentation of the Dewhurst Cup (named after a chain of butcher shops whose slogan was 'we are the master butchers') in abstantio to the surgeon selected for his efforts which had singled him out for the appellation of 'The master butcher of the year'. This always seemed to go to one same particular, unfortunate doctor.

Many of our research registrars were from overseas. I can recall telling a bright young Hungarian registrar that his country had a reputation for being sharp and inventive. I told him that 'we thought of a Hungarian as a person who went into a revolving door after you and came out before you'. 'Ah', he said, 'that is only true when the other person is English'. His reply illustrated my point.

Many of our research registrars went on to run their own research departments in their home countries It was largely due to the strong bonds of friendships and mutual respect we cemented when trying out new ideas that when I retired parties were arranged for me in Hong Kong, Stanford and Sydney.

A Consultant Anaesthetist

Before I took the Chair of Anaesthesia in London University, held at Westminster and Charing Cross Medical Schools-later to be integrated into Imperial College of Medical Science, I was a consultant anaesthetist. Although my part time contract was held by the Westminster Hospital I was allowed two half days, out of a five and a half day week, in which to carry out private practice. I enjoyed these sessions enormously. Not only did they provide the money for the children's school fees but in private practice one had the time to spend getting to know the patients. Unlike the NHS where, increasingly, the patient's fitness is assessed by a nurse at a pre operative clinic, I had the time, not only to examine the patients but also to talk to them, discuss their fears and tell them about measures we might take to relieve post operative discomfort. On at least four occasions I picked up a previously undiagnosed cancer in the patient and several times I found other serious medical problems that had been overlooked. It is doubtful if they would have come to light using a nurse run questionnaire.

It was usual for me to introduce myself to the patient on entering his room, On one occasion, having done this,

I turned to the young lady who was sitting close to patient X with the words 'Mrs X I presume' only to see her blush scarlet. The patient turn to me and whispered in my ear 'I wouldn't presume if I were you- don't tell my wife'. I covered my embarrassment as best I could and resolved to be more circumspect in the future.

I learnt early on that it was a good idea to have a nurse accompany me when examining a female patient. It was on a day when the nursing staff were exceptionally busy that I went to examine a well known female singer. On entering her room I discovered her stark naked under a single sheet. I declined her pressing offer to teach me the steps of the Watutsi dance and made a hasty retreat. I can still recall her laughter at my rapid retreat.

Inevitably there are unplanned moments of panic and hilarity, especially in private practice. There was the occasion when I failed to realise that the patient was wearing false eye lashes until, on removing the face mask, I noticed one set was missing. Faced with the prospect of sending the young lady back to her bed looking lopsided I searched for many minutes but to no avail. The missing eye lashes were impossible to spot on the terrazzo floor of the operating theatre

On another occasion I was helping to lift a patient, a famous band performer, onto the operating table when something terrible happened to his head-it was as if it had split open. It took a few moments to realise that he had been wearing a full head wig which had come off revealing a totally bald head underneath.

During the time I spent in Holland I picked up a few words of Dutch. I was sufficiently fluent to wish a Dutch patient a 'good sleep' as the anaesthetic started to work. However, I was totally unprepared for the patient to wake up talking to me in Dutch as though resuming a conversation that had been temporally interrupted.

There was only one occasion when a patient I was anaesthetising remembered snatches of conversation whilst he was being operated upon. It happened in Stanford when I was on emergency duty. Norman Shumway had received a patient desperately shocked from blood loss after rupturing an abdominal aneurysm. These catastrophes are usually fatal in a matter of minutes or hours but the paramedic had put up an intravenous adrenaline drip that kept sufficient blood flowing to his vital organs to keep him alive. He was deathly pale as the adrenaline had contracted the blood vessels supplying his skin. I quickly established a life saving blood transfusion into a major vein in his groin whilst Shumway pulled on a pair of surgical gloves without first changing out of his outdoor clothes or 'scrubbing up'. The only hope of saving the patient's life was to quickly find the leak in the aorta and to clamp it to prevent further blood loss. The patient was icy cold and his pulse was barely perceptible. As I administered oxygen to try to keep him alive, Shumway made a wide deep cut on his abdomen, put in his hand into his belly and squeezed the leaking aorta to stem the blood loss. Eventually the aorta was repaired and, miraculously, the patient recovered. There is no doubt he was awake as Shumway made his incision. He never complained of any pain from the incision but he was curious about what he heard; 'why' he asked did Dr Shumway say 'here goes another live autopsy'.

There is no doubt that having the time to talk to patients before an operation is of great benefit, the patient becomes a person instead of being just 'number' on an operating list.

This benefit is reinforced by seeing the patients post operatively. Unless the doctor has the time and ability to see the results of one's administrations it is likely that any ill effect of an anaesthetic will be missed. How can one claim that a particular new technique or drug is beneficial if one does not see one's patients for oneself after the operation? It was this opinion that brought me into conflict with the Hospital management. I refused to anaesthetise any patient that I, or my assistant, had not seen. To see a patient for the first time in the anaesthetic room put pressure upon the anaesthetist to go ahead with a procedure, that might have been better delayed, for fear of causing the patient the emotional and physical distress. Fortunately, as a University employee I could not be sacked for questioning the wisdom of the non-medical managers. It may be efficient but it is bad medicine. It was evident that, in the view of the managers, I was becoming a 'grumpy old man'.

Retirement

In the Spring of 2008, unbeknown to me, my obituary appeared in the Australian press. Perhaps it was a gentle reminder that I had been around too long. I was completely unaware of my premature demise until one day, after attending a memorial service to a colleague, I came face to face with a friend who used to be the Professor of Anaesthetics in Sydney. On seeing me he went ashen as he stared at me in evident disbelief before blurting out 'I thought you were dead'. The story of the obituary came out slowly as he regained his composure. It was some weeks later that I received a letter of fulsome apology from the source of my death notice; the Australian Society of Anaesthesia. In spite of this my name seemed to have been removed from the list of Honorary Fellows as I ceased to receive copies of their proceedings after this event.

Having an official letter from a professional body to tell me that I was still alive was reassuring but at the same time it left an uncomfortable feeling that there is someone out there waiting for confirmation that they were not far out in their timing. One can see their point, by now, I have been retired for some years.

Speaking to my colleagues, nearly all look forward to retirement. I felt an enormous sense of relief at having survived a forty year stint at the sharp end of medicine, where decisions made on the spur of the moment can make the difference between a patient's life and death. Not having a major catastrophe on one's conscious is an achievement. It is also an encouragement to quit whilst one is ahead. In today's litigious world where patients are encouraged to complain about any and every aspect of their treatment, many of my friends and colleagues have undergone the mental torture associated with being a victim of a spurious and in some cases malicious complaint. Nearly all complaints lead to the doctor being suspended whilst the cause of the complaint is being investigated There is no allowance for mistakes or errors in a life or death specialty like anaesthesia and Intensive Care. So it is a great relief when most anaesthetists reach the retirement age of 65 without a blot on their reputation. Few are tempted to sign on for more active service although some succumb to become committee fodder rather than spend their lives at home doing the washing up.

I was fortunate in being offered the post of research adviser to the prestigious Royal National Orthopaedic Hospital before I actually had retired. I had been involved in clinical orthopaedic surgery during the latter years at the Chelsea and Westminster Hospital and it was a burgeoning specialty by virtue of the number of joints that the human skeleton possess and the ingenuity of technicians to invent joint replacements for them when they became diseased or just worn out. However my particular interest was with spinal injuries. I had long been convinced, from my work with the nervous innervations of muscle, that with modern scientific techniques it should be possible to achieve a better recovery of function after a catastrophic spinal injury. Even if this were only marginal it might help some of these young people to live a more independent and dignified life. It was a very much a part time job that offered just the sort of work I enjoyed and also left me time to continue with my teaching and lecturing commitments.

One of those commitments was to write a chapter for the American 'Harold Wood Museum' book of the year. This organisation has been a chronicler of anaesthetic history for many years. It produces a series of books which have created a living record of the major events and personalities that have influenced anaesthesia. On this occasion they asked five eminent anaesthetists, who were at retirement age, from three continents, to record their memories of the effect of the changes they had witnessed. I was selected to represent Europe. The book makes fascinating reading, all of us more or less agreed that we had indeed been one of the lucky generation. We had witnessed a time of rapid change as new technologies and drugs allowed us to meet the challenges of the new surgical procedures that were introduced Our working lives covered an era when operative mortality fell from 1 in 2,000 to 1 in 250-350,000, largely due to improvements in anaesthesia and post operative care. It had been an exciting and rewarding time. We all looked into the future with apprehension convinced that the new generation of doctors would neither have the same opportunities as we had enjoyed nor are they likely to experience the thrill of seeing patients survive who in previous times would have died. It was the feeling that one's own particular experience and knowledge made a difference that made our times so rewarding. Today, anaesthesia is by rote, one is expected to rigidly follow a 'manual', any deviation invites criticism or complaint from the technicians or nursing staff. Unexpected events are treated by algorythmn, and the patient a depersonalised number in a target driven machine. The fear of litigation and censure prevents innovation, stifling new ideas and practice. Clinical research is rare and positively discouraged by a regime driven by meeting targets and costs. The number of true research papers in our journals has tumbled from around 80% of all refereed papers in 1980 to less than 15% in 2009. This represents a tremendous loss as clinical research provides the seed corn of scientific endeavours.

A Grumpy Old Man?

I suppose that I qualify for the 'Grumpy Old Man' title. I certainly look back with a feeling of nostalgia for the good old days. I do believe that today's doctors do not have the same freedom to exercise their 'know how' as we did. Much of the fun and the sense of intellectual accomplishment that we enjoyed is denied to the present generation of hospital doctors but then the times are different and require differing attitudes.

I do look back on the excitement that I felt on becoming a doctor with nostalgic longing. The altruism, the enthusiasm and, as my generation saw it, the opportunity to do something worth while to reduce suffering irrespective of patient's ability to pay that was provided by the new NHS, is missing today. The health service has become so bureaucratic, so dominated by cost efficiency, so health and safety conscious and so politically correct that hospital doctors have become demoralised, they are servants of the State rather than the patient. Their ability to treat an individual patient to the best of their ability, irrespective of the time it takes or the particular needs of that patient have been seriously curtailed by the need to treat patients according to authoritarian schemes of what some committee has decided is the 'best practice'. Cost efficiency demands have placed severe constraints on how they apportion their time. Whilst denying a particular treatment or a particular expensive drug may be in the best interests of the community it is a violation of the unspoken contract between patient and doctor if this prevents the best treatment available being offered to a particular patient who would benefit from it. These are decisions we used to be able to make but which are denied to present day doctors.

No one can deny that stricter criteria of experimental treatments and research was needed to prevent abuse of the laise faire attitude of my days but the present ethics committee system stifles clinical research. These bodies find it easier to play safe and deny or delay approval of a particular research project, than to grant it. The right of patients to know when they are the subject of experimental tests is absolute. The nature and hazards of these should always be made clear. I have never known a patient to refuse a reasonable request to be the subject of an experiment when it has been properly explained. However, the need to explain a request to retain patient tissue, whether it be blood, sputum or a biopsy, before the tissue or specimen has been obtained, has become applied in a ludicrously restrictive fashion. As many of these studies are retrospective, made after the patient has been diagnosed and treated, it becomes impossible to comply with the restrictions that have been imposed.

Although I was taught, from my earliest days as a trainee, to keep records of my anaesthetic techniques, a chore that has become easier with automated recording devices, many centres regarded record keeping as optional. Today it is, rightly, a mandatory requirement. However, in emergency situations when one is concentrating on saving a patient's life, it is unreasonable to demand the same detailed notes be taken, yet a failure to do so is now considered negligent. The accuracy of the record has become more important than saving a patient's life.

Like most of my colleagues I worked absurdly long hours, especially during my training period. For the most part, we did so because we loved what we were doing, we wanted the experience and our hard work was recognised. By diligence and by attention to the needs of our patients we received preferment in our climb up the ladder to the eventual rank of consultant. The harder we worked the better our prospects. As a consultant a good salary and standard of living was to be anticipated even if few aspired to a Rolls Royce and chauffer type of life.

Today, doctors work regulated shifts, the total hours they can work is limited, they have few qualms about leaving a patient half way through treatment or operation and handing over to a colleague. Their pattern of work is similar to that of a shop assistant. Provided they are not actually totally callous or negligent, in their approach to the patients, it does not affect their promotion which, in most instances, depends more on 'Buggins turn' than patient care or hard work.

As a 'Grumpy Old Man', what saddens me is that the present day practitioners have lost so much of the intellectual satisfaction enjoyed by those of my generation. They have surrendered their ability to treat their patients as they think best and instead they have succumbed to being civil servants, mindless administrators of state injunctions. In return for a less stressful and better paid lifestyle they have accepted a restriction of their freedom to act as professional doctors. They are no longer the inheritors of the vision of A.J. Cronin's hero in the Citadel, or of those of us who had such high hopes of a new era for medicine, when we qualified as doctors, in the then new National Health Service.